Sanchez:

A Christmas Carol

Anonymous

This short Christmas story is for all the friends I met in Paris, for all the friends of the Bourbon Kid on Facebook and for John in Ohio who likes Sanchez as much as I do.

Novels by Anonymous –

The Book With No Name (2007)
The Eye of the Moon (2008)
The Devil's Graveyard (2010)
The Book of Death (2012)
Sanchez: A Christmas Carol (2014)
The Red Mohawk (2015)
The Plot to Kill the Pope (2016)

"This one is just for fun."

Anonymous.

Cover jacket designed by Adam Barringer

One

Sanchez hated many things, such as strangers, going to church, bus rides and snowfall. But one thing he hated above all else was being woken in the middle of a dream. Especially when it was a good one, like the one he was having right now, where he was Bruce Willis in *Die Hard*. One minute he was engaging in witty repartee while shooting bad guys, and the next he was lying awake staring at the ceiling in his bedroom, trying to figure out what the noise was that had woken him.

It took a while to recognize it and it wasn't a noise he would have expected to hear in his bedroom in the middle of the night.

Rattling chains!

His initial reaction was to try and get back to sleep, but no matter how hard he tried, the sound of the rattling chains was still evident. And it was getting louder.

He rolled over onto his side and saw Flake's side of the bed was empty again. She had been staying in an apartment near her workplace on a regular basis in recent times. He missed her being around, not least of all because in her absence he had to make his own breakfast in the mornings.

It had been three months since she started working at Waxwork Tower. She had come home regularly in the beginning but lately her trips back to The Tapioca had become less and less frequent.

But the persistent rattling of the chains! What the fuck was it all about?

'Sanchez, *Sanchez*.' A creepy voice cried out his name from somewhere nearby. He recognized the voice too. It was an old lady's voice, croaky in tone. A voice he hadn't heard in years. 'Sanchez, *woo, wooo*.'

He sat bolt upright.

It was the Mystic Lady's voice. The annoying fortune-teller that used to travel around Santa Mondega in a caravan. She had particularly irritated Sanchez over the years by turning up wherever he went.

As he rubbed his eyes he caught sight of a faint silhouette of the old fortune-telling hag standing at the end of his bed. She was dressed the same as ever, a shitty old grey cardigan over a black dress. Her hair was greyer than he remembered too. And so was her face. She was still fucking ugly though.

Then it hit him. He was seeing everything in black and white. Just like a dog!

He squinted and shook his head. *Still no colour.* He stared hard at the Mystic Lady. She had a set of heavy metal chains draped around her shoulders and a big metal ball chained around her left ankle.

'What the fuck are you doing here?' Sanchez asked.

'Sanchez, woo, woo,' the Mystic Lady repeated, waving her arms wildly in the air and accidently hitting herself in the chin with her chains.

'Will you quit with the stupid ghost noises? And stop waving your arms, I'm getting a whiff of your armpits.'

The Mystic Lady stopped gesticulating and edged closer to the bed. She sat down on the end of it and leant towards him.

Sanchez recoiled and pulled the sheets up to his neck. 'All right steady on. That's close enough.'

'You're in trouble Sanchez. I've been sent to warn you.'

'Why is everything in black and white?'

The Mystic Lady looked surprised by the question. After a brief pause for thought, she shrugged. 'I don't know. For effect I suppose.'

'I'm going to turn on the lights then.'

'No, don't. I'll disappear if you switch on the lights.'

'All the more reason why I should do it then. This is clearly a dream. And if I might say, it's not a very good one.'

'This is no dream Sanchez.'

'Really? Then why am I wearing a nightcap?'

It hadn't been lost on him that for the first time in his life he was wearing a floppy nightcap on his head. He would never normally consider wearing a such a garment. He didn't even own one.

'Fine,' said the Mystic Lady. 'Get up and turn the light on. But let me first point out that the nightcap is the only thing you're wearing.'

Sanchez pulled the bed sheets up a little further, right up to his chin. 'Go on then. Let's get this over with. What do you want?'

'I've come to warn you of what lies ahead.'

'Oh God, you're not moving in are you? If you're planning on haunting me I'll tell you now, I've seen *Poltergeist* and *The Exorcist*. I'll get someone round to have you evicted.'

The Mystic Lady sighed. 'No, I'm here to tell you that over the course of the next twenty-four hours you will be visited by three ghosts. The ghost of Christmas past, the ghost of Christmas present and the ghost of Christmas yet to come.'

'Excellent,' Sanchez replied sarcastically. 'Well I'll look forward to that. Are you finished?'

'I'm not sure.'

Sanchez laid back down, slamming his head into the pillow and closing his eyes. He pulled the sheets over his head and tried to get back to his original *Die Hard* dream before it was too late. He'd barely closed his eyes when he heard the sound of the chains rattling again. It went on for about ten seconds before it stopped suddenly. Sanchez opened his eyes. He lifted the sheet from his head and peered out from under it. The Mystic Lady was standing by the side of the bed staring down at him.

'What now?' he snapped.

'There's more.'

'Of course there is,' Sanchez sighed. 'It's never straightforward with you is it?'

'I'm here to warn you that if you don't change your ways before midnight on Christmas Eve you will lose Flake for ever.'

Sanchez bolted upright again. 'What do you mean?'

'The three ghosts who come to visit you will show you what your life was like before you met Flake, what it is like now, and what it will be like if you don't change your ways.'

'Change my ways? Why do I need to change my ways?'

'Well you could stop pouring piss into people's drinks you know. Flake doesn't like that. In fact no one does. It's unhygienic and most of all it's just very unpleasant.'

'It's pretty funny though.'

'I don't think so and nor does Flake. And she knows you've been doing it to customers when she's not looking. It's one of the reasons she started working at the waxworks, instead of helping out in the Tapioca.'

'She never said that was the reason.'

'She shouldn't have to.'

'Why not?'

'Because she shouldn't.'

'That's not a reason.'

'Yes it is, and it's not even the *only* reason. You should have agreed to go with her to her office Christmas party tomorrow night.'

'Why would I want to go to a waxwork company's Christmas party?'

'Because it was important to Flake. You need to stop being so selfish all the time. If you don't want to lose her you have to go to her Christmas party tomorrow night and show her you're willing to change. Make a grand gesture or something.'

'Like what?'

'Watch *Jerry Maguire*.'

'How's that a grand gesture?'

'It's not. You should watch it because it could give you some inspiration. Steal some ideas from it and use them to win back Flake.'

'Stealing ideas from movies? That sounds lame.'

The Mystic Lady sighed. 'If you do it well, no one will even notice. Just learn some of the romantic lines and recite them to Flake when you see her.'

Sanchez wasn't convinced. '*Jerry Maguire though?* Seriously? Can't I just quote some lines from Scarface instead? I've seen that a bunch of times. It's got some great quotes in it, like *"Say hello to my little friend!"'*

The Mystic Lady rattled her chains and lumbered back to the end of the bed. Sanchez caught a waft of mothballs from her dirty old cardigan and screwed up his nose.

'You'd better do something,' she croaked. 'The three ghosts of Christmas will be at the party to show you the error of your ways. If you pay attention to what they say maybe you'll learn something.'

Sanchez waved a dismissive hand. 'I don't believe any of this. First of all this is a dream.'

'Maybe.'

'And second of all, you're a fucking useless fortune-teller. You only ever got the unimportant stuff right. Fifty percent of your predictions were wrong. I'll bet that's what got you killed.'

The Mystic Lady looked unimpressed. 'Sanchez,' she said, rattling her chains once more for no particular reason. 'If you don't want to end up like me you'll follow the yellow brick road tomorrow. It will lead you to Flake's Christmas party. If you don't go you will be doomed for all eternity, just like me.'

'There's no yellow brick road in Santa Mondega, you daft cow.'

'It's a metaphor, dickhead.'

'A *meta-what?*'

'Be ready at 8 o'clock tomorrow night. You will receive a phone call from the driver. When he asks you where you want to go, you tell him to take you to Waxwork Tower. He'll wait outside for you for five minutes, no more, no less. Then he'll leave. Make sure you're in the car with him.'

The Mystic Lady waved her arms around a little more and made some *"wooing"* noises for effect, before eventually vanishing in a puff of smoke.

Sanchez breathed a sigh of relief and went straight back to sleep.

9

Two

Sanchez woke up in the morning and discovered he was still wearing the nightcap that had been on his head during the Mystic Lady's visit. As he rolled out of bed, he discovered he was still naked too, which was odd because he normally slept in his boxer shorts. He spotted them on the floor near the door next to an empty bottle of Bacardi. An unpleasant thought crossed his mind. Could it be possible that the ghost of the Mystic Lady had swiped some free booze from the bar, gotten drunk and then debagged him while he slept? He shuddered at the thought of it. A hot shower was required.

He spent all day fretting about whether or not to go to Flake's Christmas party. The visit from the Mystic Lady had really creeped him out. Not just because she was dead either, there was something deeply unsettling about knowing that she'd possibly undressed him and interfered with him while he slept. The dirty old bag.

Her visit seemed more real every time he thought about it.

The day didn't get much better either. He rented a copy of *Jerry Maguire*, just like the Mystic Lady had suggested. He hadn't managed to watch it right to the end but it was pretty obvious that the main catchphrase from the movie was *"Show me the money"*. Quite how that was supposed to help him win back Flake he had no idea. It didn't seem like a particularly romantic thing to say to her if he had to make a grand gesture in front of all her work colleagues. Even so, he recited it over and over in his head so he wouldn't forget it. Then he watched Scarface again and decided that Al Pacino's quotes were way better than anything Tom Cruise and Cuba Gooding Junior could come up with.

He thought about what he could wear to an office Christmas party at Waxwork Tower. It would no doubt require him to dress smartly. Unfortunately Sanchez didn't own a suit so he had to do the best with what he had. He put on his best pair of pants, a black pair that had seen better days but generally hid food stains quite well. And seeing as it was fairly chilly out in the evenings he put on a string vest and slipped his favourite Christmas jumper on over it. It was one that Flake had bought for him the year before. A classic white woolly jumper with the words *"I thought you'd be bigger"*, sewn on the front, in red lettering. It was a quote from Sanchez's favourite movie *Road House*. Flake knew exactly what he liked, and she had good taste in clothes. He figured she'd be pleased to see him wearing it.

He waited nervously for eight o'clock in the evening to arrive. The Mystic Lady had told him to expect a phone call from "the driver". He still wasn't convinced the phone would ring, but he made sure it was within earshot while he watched *Bad Santa* on television.

Sure enough when eight o'clock arrived, the phone rang, just like the Mystic Lady had predicted. Sanchez switched off the television and peered out of the window. There was a car parked outside. It was a silver Chevrolet Impala with blacked out windows.

He took a deep breath and answered the phone. 'Hello Sanchez Garcia speaking.'

A voice on the other end of the line spoke softly. 'There's a hundred thousand streets in this city.'

'Are you my cab driver? Do you know where we're going?' Sanchez asked.

'You don't need to know the route.'

'Eh? Oh that's good.'

'You give me a time and a place. I give you a five minute window.'

'I want to go to the Christmas party at Waxwork Tower.'

'Anything happens a minute either side....'

Sanchez couldn't be bothered to listen to any more of the driver's nonsense, so he hung up the phone and hurried out through the front door, locking it behind him. It was cold outside and he wondered if it might be wise to wear a jacket over the vest and jumper combo. But the driver kept revving the engine on the car as if to indicate that he was becoming impatient. Sanchez remembered what the Mystic Lady had said about the driver only waiting for five minutes, so he dashed over to the back door and jumped in. As soon as he closed the door the car pulled away and immediately sped off down the road.

There was a blue tinted window separating the driver from the back seat passengers so Sanchez was unable to get a good look at the driver. All he could make out was that it was a man wearing a black jacket and a tight fitting blue baseball cap.

'Having a busy night?' Sanchez asked.

The driver didn't respond.

'Of course you are,' Sanchez continued. 'Christmas Eve. You're probably dead busy, right?'

Again no response. Sanchez considered the possibility that the tinted window separating him from the driver might be soundproofed, so he tapped on the glass. The driver glared into the rear view mirror. Sanchez was able to make out the whites of his eyes but little else. The look suggested he didn't want to talk.

'Got any Christmas music?' Sanchez shouted through the glass.

The driver pressed a button on the stereo. Some rap music started blaring out. Sanchez hated rap. And this rubbish sounded like MC Pedro, the former rapping werewolf that once had his throat ripped out in the Tapioca after upsetting the Bourbon Kid.

Sanchez sat back and peered out of the side window at the Santa Mondega skyline. The buildings were all lit up by Christmas lights that stood out brightly in the night sky. The city was a cool place to live and very scenic at night. And these days it was a relatively safe place to live since the Bourbon Kid had murdered all the vampires and werewolves, *and that bloody Mummy.*

After about fifteen minutes he saw Waxwork Tower up ahead in the distance.

'That's the place,' he said. 'Just pull up by the steps at the front entrance.'

The driver steered the car into the driveway of the Waxwork Tower estate and pulled the car up at the front entrance as instructed. The tinted window between them whirred and slid down a couple of inches. Sanchez peered over it.

'How much do I owe?' he asked.

The driver finally spoke in a deep husky voice, barely louder than a whisper. 'Twenty bucks.'

'I'll tell you what,' said Sanchez. 'Rather than pay you now, why don't you pick me up later and I'll pay you the full fare then?'

'I'll give you a five minute window.'

'Yes of course,' said Sanchez, reaching for the door to get out. 'Pick me up from here at midnight. Thanks.'

He climbed out of the car and slammed the door shut behind him. He could hear the driver rambling on something about not hanging around if Sanchez was late. Well Sanchez had no intention of still being at Waxwork Tower at midnight. He planned to get out of paying the fare by getting another cab firm to take him home. Or better still, if all went well, he'd get Flake to give him a ride home. He walked up to the front entrance of the building feeling rather pleased with himself.

The building was twelve stories high and looked impressive from the outside. It had mirrored walls and windows that shone brightly in the night sky. The glass screen doors at the front entrance opened automatically as he approached. He walked through them and up to the reception desk. A middle-aged man wearing a red tunic and white shirt was sitting behind the desk. The man had wavy brown hair and stupid thick-rimmed glasses that made his eyes look tiny. He greeted Sanchez with a warm smile.

'Good evening sir. Can I help you?'

'Yes, I'm looking for Flake Munroe.'

'You must be Sanchez Garcia?'

'That's right.'

The clerk slid a plastic card over the desk to him. 'Here, this is your guest pass, sir. Flake is up on the sixth floor. They're having a Christmas party up there to raise money for a local orphan boy called Tiny Tim.'

'Oh really?' Sanchez couldn't hide his disappointment. 'That sounds shit.'

The clerk laughed as if he thought Sanchez was joking. 'They're the only ones still in the building. The party is well underway. There's only one elevator in operation tonight, for security reasons. It's the service elevator just over there. Have a great night, sir.'

The clerk pointed to an elevator in the wall next to a staircase. It had shiny silver doors and a digital display above it that indicated it was currently on the sixth floor.

'Thanks.'

Sanchez strolled breezily along the corridor towards the elevator feeling confident about what lay ahead at the party. He was looking forward to seeing Flake. As he waited for the elevator he heard a voice whisper his name.

'Sanchez?'

The voice sounded vaguely familiar, but he couldn't quite place it. He hadn't heard it in a long time. He turned around slowly and saw a policeman, a street cop dressed in dark blue trousers, a light blue shirt and a puffy black jacket. He had jet-black hair in a naff frizzy flat top style that suggested he was trying to look like a twenty year old. He had to be in his early fifties though, in spite of the lack of wrinkles on his face. Sanchez recognized him and knew immediately that he wasn't a real cop. The clerk on the reception desk wasn't paying any attention to them. Instead he was watching a football match on a small portable television beneath his desk. The phoney cop walked right past the reception and up to Sanchez. He beckoned Sanchez in close as if he wanted to whisper something in his ear.

Sanchez frowned, unsure of whether or not he could trust this rubber-faced man disguised as a cop. 'What do you want?' he asked.

Then quietly, so that the clerk couldn't hear him, the cop uttered the words the bartender feared most. 'I'm the ghost of Christmas past.'

'No you're not. You're Nigel Powell, the judge from the *Back From the Dead* show in The Devil's Graveyard.'

'That's true. But tonight, for one night only, I'm the ghost of Christmas past.'

Three

Sanchez hadn't seen Nigel Powell in a very long time. It had been years since the Halloween holiday when he'd taken a trip to The Devil's Graveyard and stayed in Nigel's *Hotel Pasadena*. But now in spite of the fact Sanchez distinctly remembered seeing him eaten alive by zombies, the talent show judge and hotel owner was standing before him dressed as a cop.

The desk clerk still wasn't paying them any attention. Nigel spoke in a hushed tone nonetheless and leaned in close enough for Sanchez to feel the moisture on his breath as he talked.

'Sanchez, I've come to show you that you need to change your ways. I assume the Mystic Lady has already informed you that you should expect a visit from me.'

Sanchez wiped some of Nigel's spit off his face before replying. 'She blathered on about something. I certainly wasn't expecting you though. I barely know you.'

'Well I know all about you, Sanchez and I'm here to warn you that you need to change.'

'Why? What's wrong with this sweater?'

'Not the sweater, you clown. You need to change your ways, or bad things will happen to you. The ghost of Christmas present and Christmas yet to come will show you as much.'

'Bad things? Like what?'

'Karma, for all the bad things you've done.'

Sanchez recoiled in shock. '*What bad things?*'

'You want me to list them?'

'If you must.'

'Well, there's the time you pushed Robert Johnson into a giant hole in the ground that sent him all the way down to the pits of hell.'

'That was an accident!'

'But you never owned up to it when people asked you where he was.'

Sanchez raised an eyebrow. 'Pah. That doesn't change the fact it was an accident.'

'Okay. What about the time you set fire to Santa Claus in front of a group of girl scouts?'

Sanchez remembered it well. It was something he was extremely proud of, a highlight from his brief career as a cop.

'That Santa Claus was a vampire! I saved all those girls from being killed. That fat bastard would have eaten the lot of 'em.'

'Even so, setting him on fire was extreme. At least six of those girls are in therapy now because they saw that.'

'Ungrateful little bitches.'

Nigel shook his head. 'All right, look. You're losing Flake and she's the best thing that ever happened to you. Look at the Christmas present you gave her last year for example. A T-shirt with a picture of your face on it and the caption *"I'm with this guy, so hands off!'*

'That was funny. She loved it.'

'She'd have loved a pair of earrings more. Or even some flowers.'

'You don't know Flake like I do. She loves that T-shirt. She wears it all the time.'

'Yeah. Underneath a sweater when it's cold.'

Sanchez scoffed. 'Aren't you supposed to be showing me visual images of all this stuff? This all seems very low budget.'

Nigel held out a cell phone. 'Here,' he said. 'Take this. If things with Flake don't go well when you see her upstairs, give me a call. I'm an expert with the ladies. I'll give you all the advice you need to win her back.'

Sanchez looked at the phone. It was a big cheap old thing, but better than the one he currently owned and had inadvertently left at home. 'Why are you so keen to help me?' he asked.

'Because,' said Nigel, leaning in close. 'This is my chance for redemption. If I get you to change your ways, I can go up to Heaven. You see I wasn't a bad guy when I was alive, I just made a dodgy deal with the Devil.'

'Yeah, whatever. I heard all about your deal in The Devil's Graveyard. It wasn't very interesting then and no one wants to hear it again now. So if you don't mind, I'll say thank you for the phone and bid you farewell.'

Sanchez turned his back on Nigel and headed for the elevator at the end of the corridor. Nigel called out one last thing.

'I'll speak to you again soon, Sanchez. Don't forget to call me. And watch out for Wallace!'

Four

Sanchez stepped out of the elevator on the sixth floor. The party was already in full swing. There were smartly dressed people milling around pretending to be interested in each other's stories about their kids, sports cars, boob jobs and fake tans. The men were all in suits, the women mostly in cocktail dresses. Sanchez looked around for any sign of Flake. She wasn't generally one for wearing flashy dresses. He expected to see her in something classy but discreet.

He made his way through a crowd of people, all of whom seemed very merry from an abundance of free wine. There was a chubby blonde haired lady in a black and white uniform pushing a trolley of free booze around. Sanchez ignored her because he'd spotted a waiter on the far side of the room. The waiter was a silver haired fellow and he was chatting up a couple of the middle-aged female guests. Most importantly though, his trolley was loaded with sandwiches and miniature slices of pizza.

Sanchez had barely made it halfway across the room towards the food trolley when an elderly Japanese looking fellow in a smart grey suit with neatly combed grey hair grabbed him by the arm.

'Excuse me,' said the man. 'I don't know you.'

'I don't know you either, so we've got something in common. Now if you don't mind I…'

'What's your name?'

Sanchez sighed. The Japanese guy clearly wasn't going to let go of his arm any time soon. 'I'm Sanchez Garcia. I'm here looking for…'

'Flake Munroe?'

'Yes. How did you…'

The man shook Sanchez's hand. 'I'm Pat Miyagi. Owner of Waxwork Industries. Flake works for me. She's one of my absolute best discoveries of the year. Yesterday we sold one of her paintings for a thousand dollars at auction. It raised more money for the charity than any of our other pieces of art.'

'Well Flake's a hell of a good painter.'

'Yes she is,' Miyagi agreed. 'And she talks about you all the time. Speaks very highly of you.'

'Naturally,' Sanchez replied nonchalantly. 'I was actually hoping to…'

'See Flake? But of course. Come with me.'

Mr Miyagi had an annoying habit of finishing Sanchez's sentences. Sanchez was actually hoping to get his hands on some of the free pizza slices, but now he found himself being escorted away from the food and towards a corridor full of offices by an irritating Japanese git.

'You throw quite a party,' Sanchez observed as he followed Miyagi past a number of crappy little bonsai trees that lined the corridor. Miyagi stopped outside a door with the name FLAKE MUNROE on a silver nameplate. He knocked on the door.

Sanchez heard Flake call out *"Come in"* from inside the office. Miyagi twisted the handle on the door and pushed it open. He gestured for Sanchez to walk in first. Inside the office Flake was sitting behind a large oak desk tapping away on a keyboard. She had her beachy brown hair tied back in a ponytail and she was wearing a smart black sleeveless dress, one that Sanchez had never seen before. Her eyes lit up when she saw him.

'Wow, Sanchez you came!'

She jumped up from her seat and bounded around the desk to greet him. Sanchez noticed that her dress was quite short, stopping just above the knee. She looked fantastic.

Mr Miyagi stepped into the room and stopped alongside Sanchez. 'I found him wandering around on his own,' he said to Flake.

Flake grabbed Sanchez and planted a kiss on his cheek. She turned to Miyagi. 'Thanks for bringing him over, Pat.'

'No problem,' said Miyagi. 'It's time you came and joined the party you know.'

Before Flake could reply, another man in a charcoal grey suit poked his head around the door. He was in his early thirties but he had a boy band haircut, a floppy curtain style centre parting, which Sanchez suspected had been dyed black to hide a few grey streaks. He had a wispy black beard too, which revealed the occasional grey spot, making it look rather like he was wearing a dead badger on the lower half of his face.

'Hey Flake,' the man said grinning. 'Can I use your private bathroom?'

'Sure thing Wallace,' Flake replied with a cursory smile. 'Help yourself.'

Miyagi stepped aside to let Wallace through. 'I'll leave you guys to it,' he said, backing out into the corridor. 'But I expect to see you at the party in the next twenty minutes. It's time to enjoy yourself.'

With that Miyagi was gone. Wallace hurried over to the bathroom door in the corner of the office. When he reached it he hesitated for a moment then turned around and stared at Sanchez. He frowned, so Sanchez smiled politely at him. Wallace didn't exactly reciprocate the gesture. Instead he looked Sanchez up and down. His frown swiftly vanished and was replaced by a smirk. It wasn't lost on Sanchez that Nigel Powell had warned him to "*watch out for Wallace*".

'Who's the fat guy?' Wallace asked, nodding at Sanchez.

'This is Sanchez,' said Flake.

'Oh right. Nice to meet you. You know there's a guy in the main hall with free pizza slices, right?'

'I've already seen him,' Sanchez replied.

'Well tuck in buddy because the food is going fast. In fact, it's going through me quite fast too. Back in a sec.'

Wallace opened the door to Flake's private bathroom and ducked inside. For a brief moment, just before Wallace closed the door behind him, Sanchez spotted something in the bathroom, something that he had only ever dreamt about.

'Oh my God. Is that a gold toilet?' he spluttered.

'Yeah. Cool, huh?' Flake replied.

'I am *so* taking a dump in that later. I've never taken a shit in a gold toilet before. I bet it's awesome.'

'You are not stinking out my office!'

'Well that Wallace fella could be crapping in there right now.'

20

'He's most likely taking drugs,' said Flake.

'Really?'

'Yeah. He does a lot of coke to keep his energy up. He almost never sleeps. He's a real hard worker. Parties hard too.'

'He takes drugs at work? And your boss allows that sort of thing?'

'Only for Wallace. He's so good at his job that the bosses turn a blind eye to most of his behaviour.' Flake smiled at Sanchez with a look that suggested she was expecting him to say something. Unfortunately he was still coming to terms with the knowledge that she had a gold toilet, so after a short pause she asked him a question. 'So why did you decide to come?'

'Uh, well, I was considering making a special Christmas dinner tomorrow. I bought all the food. But then it occurred to me that you're such an amazing cook, that you might want to come over for Christmas and cook it for me? And we could spend the day together when you've finished doing the washing up.'

'Seriously?'

'Yeah.'

Flake didn't look too impressed by the generous offer. She scowled at him. 'How about you cook dinner for me once? Or take me out somewhere?'

'Take you out on Christmas day? Everywhere will be shut, silly.'

'My office won't be. I'm due to work tomorrow, I already told you that. I thought you'd come here to see me because you wanted to spend the evening together on Christmas Eve and meet my work colleagues.'

'Will they be serving Christmas food here tomorrow? If they are, maybe I could come here?'

Flake leaned back against her desk. 'Yes they are, but that doesn't mean you can't take me out for dinner sometimes.' She pointed at the door to her private bathroom. 'Wallace in there, he takes me out to lunch at least once a week, and he listens to what I have to say about my job. And he doesn't pour piss in people's drinks.'

'He sounds dead boring.'

21

'Well he's not. Our relationship, me and you, that's what gotten boring. You need to change Sanchez, because right now I'm beginning to see that hanging out with a guy like Wallace is more fun than hanging out with you. Quitting the Tapioca to come work here was one of the best things I've ever done. And this is the first time you've even come to see where I work.'

'I do like the fact that your boss is called Mr Miyagi.'

'See, you're barely listening to me. I'm telling you that we're on the verge of breaking up and all you can focus on is the fact that my boss is named after the guy from the Karate Kid films.'

'I can't believe you didn't tell me about him before.'

'I tried but you don't listen.'

The bathroom door opened and Wallace stepped out, wiping his nose. 'Hey guys, what you arguing about?' he asked.

'We weren't arguing,' said Sanchez.

'Did you show him the hip flask?' Wallace asked Flake.

'Umm no.'

'Hip flask?' said Sanchez.

'Yeah,' Wallace was beaming. 'Flake was awarded a gold hip flask this afternoon because one of her paintings sold for a thousand dollars at auction yesterday. Go on Flake, show him the flask.'

Flake walked back behind her desk and opened a drawer. She pulled out a shiny gold hip flask. Sanchez's eyes lit up.

'A gold hip flask? Oh my God. Can I have that?'

Flake tossed it over the desk to him. Sanchez caught it and began inspecting it. It was a genuine *Sergio Georgini* hand made classic. *The Holy Grail of hip flasks.*

'Merry Christmas,' said Flake. 'What did you get me?'

'Huh? Oh, it's a surprise,' he mumbled.

'Yeah, I'll bet.'

'Mind if I use the bathroom?' Sanchez asked, eager to fill his new hip flask with piss. He was pretty sure he could catch a few party guests out with the offer of a drink from a gold hip flask.

'Help yourself,' said Flake. 'I'm going to join the party. You coming Wallace?'

'You bet,' said Wallace with an irritating level of enthusiasm.

Sanchez bustled past Wallace on his way to the bathroom, and if he wasn't mistaken he thought he heard Wallace mutter something under his breath that sounded like, *'See ya later loser.'*

Nevertheless Sanchez ignored it. The gold hip flask was awesome. Filling it up with piss while standing over a gold toilet would be a real Christmas treat. Little did he know, but by the time he'd finished filling the flask with his special homebrew the building would be a very dangerous place to be.

Five

Flake hated to admit it, but she'd known for some time that Sanchez was never going to change. Her frequent lunch dates with Wallace had confirmed that not all men babbled on about themselves all the time. She knew Wallace had a reputation for sleeping with women in the office, and she knew he'd jump at the chance to get her into bed, but she appreciated the fact that he took time out of his day to ask her how things were, and he showed a genuine interest in her, something Sanchez hadn't been doing for a long time.

After leaving Sanchez behind to fill his new hip flask up with piss, Flake and Wallace headed to the main hall to join the party. The music was blaring out of the hall's speaker system now, much louder than it had been earlier. The party was in full flow. Quite a few of Flake's colleagues had become very merry thanks to the inexhaustible supply of free alcohol. The place smelt like the Tapioca on a Saturday night. The only thing drowning out the smell of booze was Wallace's aftershave. He regularly drowned himself in *Bijan for Men*, a cologne he had picked up from a local cowboy. It wasn't the subtlest smelling cologne, but it was very manly. Flake got a hefty waft of it as she was heading towards the buffet area when Wallace sneakily took hold of her hand and dragged her onto the dance floor.

'Come on,' he said. 'Let me show you some of my dance moves.'

Flake grinned. 'I've heard all about your dance moves. Plenty of girls around the office have talked about your technique.'

Wallace dragged her into the middle of the dance floor where several other couples were getting a little closer than they usually did during office hours. He pulled her in close. 'You won't know what all the fuss is about until you've experienced it for yourself,' he said rubbing up against her.

Flake felt her heart race. She suddenly felt short of breath. Wallace slid his arms around her waist and playfully squeezed her butt. She slid one arm over his shoulder and another round his waist. And she caught sight of him winking at someone over her shoulder. A second later the music changed. Wallace had obviously signalled the deejay because the Olivia Newton-John song "Physical" began playing. Wallace sang along to the lyrics as he began swirling Flake around with great gusto.

The man was a master on the dance floor. It was as if they'd been dance partners for years. They glided effortlessly around the other couples, their moves perfectly in sync with the music *and each other*.

During a brief instrumental interlude in the song, Wallace whispered in her ear. 'Your hair smells so good.'

Flake couldn't help but giggle. Even though he was kind of cheesy and she'd often thought of him as a bit of a sleazebag, he was pretty funny and he didn't take himself too seriously. She was so caught up in the moment that she completely forgot about everything else. She had a broad smile across her face for the first time in a long while. Lost in the moment with Wallace she eventually snapped back into reality when she realized she was staring over his shoulder at Sanchez. Sanchez was standing alone in the side corridor holding the gold hip flask and staring back at her. The pained look in his eyes as he watched her and Wallace grinding on the dance floor spoke volumes. She looked away, embarrassed, her conscience racked with guilt.

In the midst of all the drinking, dancing and loud music, Flake (and everyone else for that matter) had failed to notice a group of men who had entered the party via the service elevator in the far wall. There were seven or eight of them and they stood out from the other partygoers. When Flake finally spotted them out of the corner of her eye she was immediately intrigued. These men looked like they had been transported in from the eighties. Their hairstyles were seriously out-dated (unless you considered perms and mullets to be fashionable) and their clothes were highly inappropriate for an office party. Heavy leather jackets over woolly sweaters seemed to be the general theme. And all of them were wearing either chinos or stonewash jeans too. For reasons she would later be unable to explain, Flake was slow to notice the most obvious indicator of what these men were. They were all carrying heavy-duty machine guns, apart from one guy at the back who was dressed differently to the others. He wore a silver suit and carried a small pistol.

Before Flake could alert anyone to their arrival, they announced themselves in style. Two of them pointed their machine guns up at the ceiling and opened fire. The first person to scream was Candice, the buxom blonde waitress with the drinks trolley. Her scream was almost as loud as the gunfire. And it carried on for a few seconds after the intruders had stopped firing their weapons at the ceiling and the deejay had killed the music. The gunmen had the attention of the whole room. And once Candice's screaming stopped, they had total silence too.

The gentleman in the suit at the back of the gang stepped forward. Two of his colleagues separated to allow him through. His silver suit was shiny and new, even smarter than any of the suits Wallace owned and his black hair was slicked back like an eighties gangster. He smiled, an evil, confident smile, bordering on a psychotic grin. After an inappropriately long time spent looking extremely pleased with himself he calmly addressed his audience.

'Ladies and gentlemen my name is Marco Banucci. There is no need for alarm. My friends and I are not intending to kill anyone here unless it's absolutely necessary. Behave and do as you are told and you will all walk out of here alive. But make no mistake, if you do anything foolish you will be executed.' He paused to take a look at some of the terrified faces of his hostages, ensuring that everyone knew how serious he was. Then he continued. 'First of all I want everyone to hand over their cell phones. My colleague Klaus will come around with a bag and collect them. You will have these returned to you at the end of the evening.'

A man with a blond mullet haircut, dressed in chinos and a black polo-neck sweater began walking around with a black bin liner collecting cell phones. Flake stepped back from Wallace.

'What do you think they want?' she whispered.

'Cell phones,' Wallace replied. 'Weren't you listening?'

'No, I mean, what are they here for? I'm pretty sure these guys didn't break in here just to steal our cell phones. Is there a safe in the building that contains gold or huge sums of cash?'

Wallace shrugged. 'If there is, I've not seen it. Now can you shut up. I don't wanna piss these guys off.'

Klaus appeared in front of them and held his black bin liner open. He said nothing, but he didn't have to, he had a machine gun hanging from a strap on his shoulder. Flake handed over her cell phone without hesitation. As it dropped into the bag she noticed two of the other gunmen behind Klaus. They had headed down the corridor towards her office. In all the commotion she had forgotten about Sanchez. There was now no sign of him anywhere. He had vanished. The image of him standing in the corridor watching her dancing with Wallace flashed through her mind. She hoped she would see him again to have a chance to explain that she hadn't intended to hurt him. But she figured, knowing Sanchez he would be long gone by now. No doubt saving his own skin and not worrying about anyone else.

When Klaus had finished collecting all the cell phones in the black bin liner he tossed the bag on the floor at Marco Banucci's feet. Marco cleared his throat to grab the attention of his audience once more.

'I am looking for Pat Miyagi,' he said. 'If he is not handed to me within ten seconds I will kill someone. Do not test me on this. I will not count to eleven. One…'

To Flake's surprise, Wallace immediately stepped forward. She presumed that he was doing the honourable thing, and giving himself up, "Spartacus style" by pretending he was Pat Miyagi. But as two of the terrorists approached him, Wallace pointed at Mr Miyagi who was stood in the middle of a crowd of colleagues and shouted. 'That's him!'

Mr Miyagi looked shocked. There were gasps all round from his colleagues as the terrorists turned their attention on Waxwork Tower's top man.

Marco Banucci glanced over at Wallace. 'Thank you,' he said without an ounce of genuine gratitude in his voice. He then strolled over to Miyagi and held out his hand. 'Mr Miyagi, how nice to make your acquaintance. Come with me.'

Two of the terrorists took a hold of Miyagi. Each of them took one of his arms and together they hauled him boisterously over towards the elevator. The terrified Japanese businessman was smart enough not to struggle, but it didn't stop the terrorists from slapping him about a bit for fun. The rest of the guests watched on, most of them fearing for Miyagi as much as for themselves. Apart from one.

Wallace leant over and whispered in Flake's ear. 'See that,' he said. 'I saved all our lives there. Miyagi would never have given himself up.'

'But it looks like they're going to kill him,' Flake whispered back.

'Yep, but then I'll stand a good chance of getting his job,' said Wallace. 'And if that happens, I just might make you my best girl. Imagine that, if you play your cards right you could be sleeping with the boss of Waxwork Industries.'

Six

The sight of Flake dancing with Wallace and laughing at his jokes hurt Sanchez far more than he could ever have imagined. In one brief and uncharacteristic moment of self-awareness he realized just how foolish he had been. Flake was the best thing that had ever happened to him, and he had let her slip through his fingers, and into the clutches of a coke-sniffing weasel. He made up his mind there and then to ensure that absolutely nothing would stop him from winning her back.

He thought back to the creepy visit from the Mystic Lady and the recent encounter with Nigel Powell. They had banged on about how he had to make a grand gesture to win Flake back. *Something brave*, they'd said. Well, Sanchez decided that the best way to do that, would be to march over to Wallace and give him the George McFly line from Back To the Future. *"Hey you, get your damn hands off her!"*

He was just about to do it too, but then a bunch of psychos with weird Italian accents burst in on the party and started firing their guns in the air. Well *fuck that!* Sanchez turned on his heels and ran the hell out of there.

He raced past Flake's office and burst through a fire door at the end of the corridor. He'd taken barely three steps down the emergency stairs before he spotted another gunman a few flights down, making his way up. There was no other alternative than to head back up. He decided to run up as many flights of stairs as he could before his legs got tired. That would get him as far away from the gunmen as possible. He made it up exactly *one* flight.

Running up stairs was exhausting. He needed to find somewhere to hide out until the whole situation was over and the cops arrived. There was a fire door on the next floor with the words "7th Floor – Horror Museum" stickered on in black lettering. He grabbed the door handle and yanked it open. Behind the door was total darkness, bar from a few tiny spotlights in the ceiling. He stepped inside and allowed the fire door to swing shut behind him, which served only to make it even darker than before. He tiptoed forward running his hands along the walls in the hope of finding a light switch. The only positive thing he could take from the situation was that no one could spot him in the dark, and it was highly unlikely that anyone else was on this floor.

Eventually as his eyes grew accustomed to the dark he began to calm down a little. He was breathing erratically due to a mixture of panic and a general lack of fitness. There were all kinds of waxwork figures dotted around the room. He spotted a set of light switches on a wall next to one of the waxwork figures, so he edged over there and flicked a few of the switches. Several lights began flickering before eventually lighting up the room.

Sanchez looked around. He was in a huge open plan hall. The first thing he caught sight of was a six feet high waxwork figure right next to him. It was a creature best described as half-man, half-beaver. Ugly as hell and very furry with big teeth. The sight of it made him jump back. He forgot about the gunmen downstairs and took a moment to calm himself and take in his surroundings. There were plenty of other waxwork figures to look at. They were all hideous creatures, some he recognized from dodgy old horror movies and others were just creepy half-human, half-rodent affairs like the beaver-man.

He walked out into the middle of the hall to see if there was anything big enough to hide behind or underneath. The largest creature on display was a giant mammoth in the centre of the hall, but what he really needed was something in a corner or by the wall. A mammoth's ass was big, but it didn't compare to ducking down behind the bar in The Tapioca.

Just past the service elevator he spotted a pair of waxwork figures that looked familiar. One was a tall, pale, but suave looking gentleman in a long black cape with a red shirt underneath. His nameplate read *"Count Dracula"*. Next to Dracula was an even bigger dude with a grey face and a pair of metal bolts coming out of his temples. *"Frankenstein"*

Sanchez was considering ducking behind Frankenstein when he spotted an enormous Yeti a little further along. This thing was fucking huge. It had real thick white fur on it too. As he looked it up and down, he could have sworn he saw its eyes move. For a fleeting moment it had looked like the Yeti was eyeing him up for dinner, but then its eyes flickered and it stared straight ahead. Sanchez had to consider the fact that he wasn't thinking straight due to the shock of seeing the gunmen downstairs, so he disregarded the ridiculous possibility that the Yeti could be anything other than a waxwork like all the others. And besides, he soon forgot about it when he spotted a model called The Mad Axe-man.

The Mad Axe-man looked pretty horrible. He was an old bastard with a scruffy grey beard and a crap pair of red dungarees, but he quickly became Sanchez's favourite horror legend because, well, *he had a bloody great big axe in his hands!*

Sanchez hurried over to him and grabbed the axe. He yanked it out of the statue's feeble grip. It slid out easily. He wasn't sure if lugging an axe around with him was a smart idea or not, but he felt safer with it than without it. As he pondered how best to use it if the need arose, he spotted the elevator coming up from the floor below.

SHIT!

He hauled himself and his new axe over to the giant Mammoth in the middle of the hall and concealed himself right behind its huge ass. It was a pretty shitty place to hide, but when he heard a pinging sound from the elevator to confirm that someone had arrived, he knew he'd made the best possible decision.

He peered around the leg of the mammoth and spotted Mr Miyagi and three of the Italians (who he decided must be terrorists) exiting the elevator. One of the men was wearing a smart suit and looked like he was in charge. Sanchez couldn't see his face because there was a statue in the way. The man shoved Miyagi to the floor near the horrible Beaver-man figure. Miyagi rolled onto his back and held his hands up defensively as all three of the men loomed over him. Sanchez had seen enough. He hid himself back behind the mammoth where he figured he couldn't be seen. The men were too preoccupied with Mr Miyagi to notice him so all he had to do was avoid coughing, sneezing or farting out loud.

He heard Mr Miyagi cry out, 'What do you want from me?'

One of the terrorists replied. 'Mr Miyagi. Let me assure you, if you do not hand the boy over to us you will die.'

'Listen Mister Banucci, was it?' Miyagi replied, his voice filled with fear.

'Call me Marco,' the man replied.

'Ok, Marco. The thing I don't understand is, what do you want with the boy? I can give you all the codes to the safes here. You can take as much money as you like. The boy is worth nothing.'

'I don't want money!' Marco snapped. 'I am not a common thief. I am a kidnapper and a murderer. This orphan boy you are protecting is the heir to a small fortune. And by small fortune I mean *enormous fortune.*'

'*Tiny Tim* is the heir to a small fortune?' Miyagi sounded baffled.

'An *enormous* fortune.'

'Yes of course. But really? How?'

'Mr Miyagi, do I strike you as a fool that wants to dilly dally around explaining myself to you in the hope that the police will turn up and catch me?'

'No you do not.'

'Good then shut up and listen until you think I've finished talking.'

Miyagi did not respond, so after a brief pause and a slightly irritated sigh, Marco continued.

'Tiny Tim is the illegitimate child of my brother Patrick. Unfortunately Patrick has been diagnosed with an incurable and unidentifiable disease which will kill him within forty-eight hours.'

'I'm sorry to hear that,' said Miyagi.

'Don't be,' Marco said dismissively. 'I poisoned him and I'm absolutely over it already. You see my brother Patrick was an asshole. But, to his credit he was a very wealthy asshole. And when he dies, according to his will, all his wealth will be passed on to me unless he has an heir. Until recently no one knew who his heir was, or where to find him, but evidence came to light recently, which confirms that his heir is in fact this young lad Tiny Tim. But lucky for me, if the little bastard dies, I inherit everything. So I'm sure you can now see my predicament.'

'But he's just a kid!'

'Then he'll be easy to kill.'

Miyagi sounded horrified. 'You can't seriously be intending to kill Tiny Tim? He's only ten years old.'

'I am aware of that,' said Marco. 'As I am also aware of the fact that you have him somewhere in this building. Hand him over to me or I will have no choice but to kill you.'

'He could be anywhere,' Miyagi blustered. 'I don't know which floor he's on. You know what kids are like, they wander off.'

'I'm going to count to three, there will not be a four. If you haven't told me where he is, I'm going to kill you. Do you understand?'

'I don't know where he is.'

'One.'

'I'm telling you the truth.'

'Two.'

'I think he's gone home already.'

BANG!

Sanchez heard the sound of blood and brain splattering onto the floor. His curiosity got the better of him and he peered around the mammoth's leg again, just in time to see the body of Mr Miyagi laid out on the floor. His head flopped to one side and his eyes rolled up in his head. His tongue lopped out onto the floor. There was a gaping hole in his forehead, with blood spurting out of it. It reminded Sanchez of the time he'd seen a dead Otis Redding impersonator in an elevator, which in turn reminded him of his own amazing *Shitting on the Dock of the Bay* joke. A classic.

He watched Marco Banucci kick Miyagi's corpse a couple of times for good measure before he turned back to his two buddies and spoke. 'Right,' he said. 'It looks like we'll have to start searching the building for Tiny Tim. Whoever finds him gets a million bucks. But first of all, before you get started, get rid of this idiot's body.'

As Sanchez watched the dead body of Mr Miyagi being dragged into the elevator, he pondered the possibility of finding Tiny Tim himself. Maybe he could get the million bucks if he found the kid and handed him over to the terrorists? He quickly dismissed the idea. Of far greater concern was the possibility that the terrorists might kill more of their hostages, *like Flake.*

Seven

After the terrorists dragged Mr Miyagi's body away and took the elevator back down to the party, Sanchez pondered his options. He needed to alert the police to what was going on. And almost as importantly, he needed to grab a bite to eat. He could still visualize the pizza slices that were available downstairs. The Meat Feast pizza had looked particularly inviting. And Sanchez was so hungry he would even have considered the vegetarian option. This was a serious crisis.

He stepped out from behind the giant Mammoth's butt and surveyed the room. There was no one else in sight, just a trail of blood that led over to the elevator. He reached into his pocket and pulled out the cell phone Nigel Powell had given him. The display said something about EMERGENCY CALLS ONLY. Well, his need for pizza was definitely an emergency. His rumbling stomach was a constant reminder.

Sanchez was no expert with cell phones. There were way too many options and applications, so he had rarely used his for anything other than making calls to the local pizza place. He knew the number for *Fat Frank's Pizzas* off by heart and fortunately their policy was *"We deliver in times of need, without fail"*. And their advert on local TV showed a guy dressed in black delivering a pizza to a prisoner of war behind enemy lines, so a mere terrorists takeover at Waxwork Tower should be within their remit. Unfortunately when Sanchez dialled the number, he found to his dismay that instead of the call going straight through to *Fat Frank's*, the display came up with a message saying REDIRECTING. He put the phone to his ear. It was ringing, but he had no idea who he was being put through to. After less than two rings a woman's voice answered.

'Hello, emergency services. How may I help you?'

Sanchez frowned. 'Is Fat Frank there?'

'No this is emergency services.'

'Okay, lady,' he said. 'Couple of things. First of all, some terrorists seem to have taken over Waxwork Tower. Could you send some cops to sort it out please? They've already murdered one hostage and it sounds like they're looking for someone called Tiny Tim.'

'Is this a joke?'

'No. Mr Miyagi is already dead. I just saw him get waxed. And there's a whole bunch of hostages on the sixth floor.'

'Sir this line is reserved for emergency calls only.'

'Well I didn't phone you intentionally, I was actually just trying to order a pizza! But for some reason my call was diverted through to you. Now, seeing as I'm here and doing *you* a favour by reporting this terrorist takeover perhaps you could have the good grace to put me through to *Fat Frank's.*'

'Is that Sanchez from The Tapioca?'

'Yes. Who's that?'

'Jennifer Dickinson. You served me a rather foul tasting ginger ale once, remember?'

'Not particularly. Look Miss Dickinson, if you don't send some cops here and put me through to Fat Frank you're going to have the deaths of some innocent people on your conscience. And I get real cranky when I haven't eaten.'

He heard Jennifer Dickinson sigh on the other end of the line. 'Okay I'll send a couple of guys to check this out, but if this turns out to be a prank just remember, I know who you are.'

The line went dead. The bitch had hung up on him without putting him through to Fat Frank's. Sanchez was livid. His stomach was making all kinds of weird noises now too. As luck would have it he spotted a vending machine in the corner of the hall. He picked up his axe and dashed over to it. It was potentially the greatest vending machine of all time. It was loaded up with Twinkies, donuts and chocolate bars, as well as a selection of fizzy drinks in cans. He reached into his pocket and pulled out a five-dollar bill. That was when he spotted the sign that said, NO CASH. DINER CARDS ONLY.

There was only one thing for it. He was going to have to smash the glass with his axe. He lifted the axe over his shoulder. The darned thing suddenly felt a lot heavier than before. He swung it down hard on the glass display at the front of the vending machine. *Bingo!* The axe crashed through the glass with ease.

Unfortunately before he had even taken the nearest Twinkie, an alarm bell starting ringing out loud.

Really loud.

Fucking Loud in fact.

Shit!

Sanchez put the axe down on the floor and snatched a Twinkie out of the vending machine. Time was in short supply so he only had time to grab two donuts to accompany the Twinkie. As he was considering whether to grab a can of fizzy drink too, he heard another noise behind him. The gears on the elevator began moving again. Someone was coming. He dashed back over to the Mammoth and repositioned himself behind it again. And he started chomping on a splendid donut with pink icing.

The damned alarm carried on ringing, so he couldn't tell if the elevator had stopped on his floor or not. He was on the verge of going deaf when the alarm did eventually stop ringing. Fortunately his eardrums were still intact because he could hear himself chewing his donut. He listened carefully for the sound of any intruders on the floor. He heard footsteps and then a man's voice spoke out. He had an Italian accent.

'You can come out,' the man said. 'I won't hurt you.'

Sanchez stayed deadly silent. He even stopped chewing his donut for a few seconds.

'I can see you back there behind the Mammoth,' the man continued. 'Come out, slowly.'

Fuck.

Sanchez swallowed the remainder of his donut, before responding. 'I'm unarmed!' he called out, suddenly regretting the fact he had left the axe by the vending machine.

He heard the man adjusting a machine gun, preparing for the possibility of using it.

'Who are you?' the man called out.

Sanchez raised his hands in surrender and stepped out from behind the Mammoth. He was greeted by the sight of a burly, blond man wearing a blue sweatshirt and black jeans and pointing a machine gun at him.

'I'm Sanchez Garcia. I'm just a bartender.'

'Prove it,' the man said. 'Show me some ID.'

Sanchez reached slowly for his wallet, not wanting to make any sudden movements that might cause the guy to get an itchy trigger finger. He pulled it out from his back pocket.

'Throw it over here,' said the man.

Sanchez tossed it to him. The man caught it and opened it, all the while keeping his gun and one eye trained on Sanchez. He flicked through the wallet and pulled out one of the ID cards.

'It says here you are a policeman,' he said, his face revealing a look of concern.

'Oh, that's nothing,' said Sanchez. 'I was on the police force for about two days once, during a crisis. I just keep the badge to impress chicks, you know.'

'Bullshit,' the blond guy snapped. 'Who sent you? How many of you are there here?'

'Seriously, it's just me.'

'So why did you sound the alarm?'

'I didn't mean to,' said Sanchez reaching into his pocket for the Twinkie. 'I broke into the vending machine for this.'

'Bullshit. No one's that stupid!'

'It's a *Twinkie*, man,' Sanchez protested. 'Have you ever tried one? They're amazing.'

'I don't believe you. You wouldn't steal from a vending machine. You're a policeman. There are rules for policemen. One of them is *don't steal.*'

'Well, like I said, I'm not a policeman any more. Keep up.'

'Shut up!'

The man tossed Sanchez's wallet back at him and reached for a walkie-talkie on his belt. He put it to his mouth and spoke into it. 'Marco, it's Klaus. I'm on the seventh floor investigating that alarm that just went off. It turns out we've got an undercover cop up here. He's the one who set off the alarm. What do you want me to do with him?'

Marco's voice came through loud and clear. Just two simple words.

'Kill him.'

Eight

Five minutes after the terrorists had dragged Mr Miyagi off to the sixth floor, a loud gunshot rang out from above. It made Flake shudder and it generated a number of gasps and squeals from the other hostages who were huddled together in a group on the floor where only minutes earlier they had been happily dancing the night away.

Flake nudged Wallace. 'I think they killed Miyagi,' she whispered.

Wallace nodded in agreement. 'Yep, well, either him, or your friend Sanchez.'

'What makes you think they've found Sanchez?' Flake asked.

'What makes *you* think they *haven't?*' Wallace said scornfully. 'He's hardly inconspicuous.'

A cold flush washed over Flake. 'Don't say things like that.'

'Okay,' said Wallace. 'Maybe they found Tiny Tim then.'

In the midst of all the horror, Flake had forgotten about Tiny Tim. The young lad was supposed to be the guest of honour at the Christmas party because he had won an award for bravery. Doctors had told him that he would never be able to walk because of a crippling spinal disease, but he had overcome it and taught himself how to walk without any aid. As reward Waxwork Industries had raised a hundred thousand dollars to pay for a spinal operation that would allow him to grow like a normal kid.

To keep Tim entertained before his presentation Flake had taken him up to a special cinema room on one of the higher floors earlier in the evening and left him watching *The Lion King*. She hoped he was still there, or had heard the gunfire and found somewhere to hide.

A pinging sound from the elevator snapped Flake back to her current predicament. She craned her neck to see if she could get a look at who was inside as the doors opened. Marco Banucci stepped out. Two of his henchmen followed him, dragging the dead body of Mr Miyagi out with them. They tossed him onto the floor so that everyone could see. Candice the waitress screamed in horror, a scream that was almost loud enough to shatter glass. Miyagi had been shot in the head. There was a gaping hole in his forehead and a huge chunk of the back of his head had been blown off. His previously impeccably combed grey hair was now matted together with chunks of blood and brain. If there was anyone who hadn't been scared before they sure as shit were scared now.

Marco Banucci raised his hand in the air to call for calm. 'Ladies and gentlemen,' he declared. 'As you can see, Mr Miyagi will not be joining us for the rest of his life.'

A tiny Japanese lady sitting near the elevator raised her hand. Flake recognized her. It was Dawn from the accounts department, or *Asian Dawn* as she was known to her colleagues. She was fairly new and was a renowned know-it-all around the office.

Marco looked at her and sneered. 'What do you want?'

'That doesn't make sense,' said Dawn, lowering her hand. 'What doesn't?'

'You said, Mr Miyagi won't be joining us for the rest of his life.'

'Yes.'

'But he's dead. So surely you should have said he won't be joining us for the rest of *our* lives.'

Marco frowned and then looked around at his henchmen. They all shrugged. Marco reached inside his suit jacket and pulled out his pistol. He pointed it at Dawn and without hesitating he squeezed the trigger.

BANG!

The bullet flew out of the gun's chamber and straight into the centre of Dawn's face. Her body slammed backwards onto the floor. Blood gushed out onto the floor, which caused Candice to scream again, although this time she had the good sense to cut it short.

Marco looked around at his audience. 'Anyone else want to raise their hand to make a pedantic remark?' he asked.

No one moved.

'Good,' he continued. 'These two dead fools will just be the first of many if we don't get what we want.'

Marco had everyone's attention. The man certainly knew how to work a room and having two dead bodies as evidence that he was a psychopath certainly helped.

'I'm looking for a boy named Tiny Tim,' he continued. 'Someone in this room must know where he is. Give him up and you will all go free. Once I have him in my possession this will all be over. You will *all* be allowed to go home to your families and carry on living your lives. But for every ten minutes that passes where I don't get Tiny Tim, I will execute another hostage. Now, does anyone want to tell me where I can find Tiny Tim, please?'

Nobody spoke up. There was only one person in the room who knew where Tiny Tim was. And that was Flake.

Nine

Klaus replaced his walkie-talkie on his belt and smiled at Sanchez. 'It looks like our time together is at an end,' he sneered.

'Did your boss just tell you to kill me?' Sanchez asked.

'He's not my boss.' Klaus flicked the safety catch off on his machine gun and pointed it at Sanchez. 'Any last requests?' he asked.

Sanchez shrugged. 'Don't kill me?'

'Nice try. Say Good night *asshole*.'

'Good night asshole!'

Klaus looked somewhat baffled by Sanchez's apathy. But that was because he didn't know what Sanchez had seen behind him. There was a giant Yeti sneaking up on Klaus. It had crept up on him while he was on the phone. And it had even placed its finger over its mouth and winked at Sanchez, so he had to consider the probability that it was on his side. Besides, if a fucking giant abominable snowman wants to be your buddy and save your life, why fight it, right?

As the Yeti reached out and grabbed Klaus's head, Sanchez closed his eyes.

CRACK!

He counted to three and then heard a gentle thud, which he assumed was the body of Klaus hitting the floor. He opened his eyes one at a time and saw Klaus lying dead on the floor. His legs were spread in a weird pose that made it look like he was trying to run across the floor. His neck had been broken by the big fucking Yeti.

Sanchez looked up at the big dude in the Yeti costume, who was in the process of peeling off his head mask. Beneath the fearsome white mask was the face of a man from Sanchez's past.

The man ripped off the rest of the Yeti outfit as Sanchez watched on, hoping to God that he wasn't naked underneath it. Fortunately, beneath the costume the man was dressed from head to toe in blue denim. The jacket was sleeveless and showed off his enormous tattooed biceps. He had long brown hair, which had gone a bit crap underneath the Yeti mask, giving him an awful "hat hair" look, not that Sanchez felt the need to mention it. But, the man's trademark that distinguished him from most other people was the single black leather glove he wore on his right hand.

It was *Rodeo Rex*. The greatest bare-knuckle fighter Sanchez had ever seen. It had been a few years since they'd last met, but Sanchez was pretty damn sure he could call Rex a friend.

Rex held out his gloved hand. 'Hey Sanchez. How's tricks?'

Sanchez grasped the gloved hand and tried to give a firm handshake. Underneath the leather glove Rex possessed a fully functional metal hand. Its grip on Sanchez wasn't gentle either, not that he dared to complain. No wonder the terrorist guy was dead. Rex could snap a man's neck in half a second. But what the fuck was he doing in Waxwork Tower on Christmas Eve?

'Rex?' Sanchez said, failing to mask his surprise. 'I thought you were dead. What the fuck?'

'And I thought you'd be bigger,' said Rex, nodding at Sanchez's jumper that had the phrase "*I thought you'd be bigger*" written across the front of it.

'Oh, cool jumper, huh?' said Sanchez proudly. 'Flake bought it for me.'

'It's nice. Looks a bit tight though, or is that the point of it?'

Sanchez hadn't considered the possibility that the slogan was anything other than a quote from Road House. 'Well yes, enough about my jumper. I heard you were dead. What happened?'

Rex nodded. 'I was dead, for a while, but now I'm the ghost of Christmas present. Looks like I got here just in the nick of time too. Did you shit yourself yet?'

'Nearly,' said Sanchez. 'But how are you here? I don't get it?'

'The Mystic Lady told you I was coming, right?'

Sanchez thought back to what the old hag had said. He didn't remember much of it, just the *woo-woo-woo-ing* and the musty smell. 'Well, she said all kinds of rubbish. I thought it was a dream though. That old bag.'

'Well, it wasn't.'

'So what's going on then? Are you dead or not?'

'I was. But I made a deal with *The Man In Red*. I work for the other side now, hunting down the undead.'

'Undead?' Sanchez pointed at Klaus's corpse. 'Was he a vampire?'

Rex shook his head. 'No. He's a normal guy, but I get Christmas week off from hunting the undead. So I'm here in Santa Mondega to help you deal with these scumbag terrorists.'

'Cool. God bless *The Man In Red* and his Christmas vacation policy.'

Rex rolled his eyes. 'Never mind about *The Man In Red*. I'm here to show you that you could lose Flake if you don't change your ways. She's downstairs right now in a room full of terrorists and terrified hostages. She's scared too and the only person there to comfort her is that weasel Wallace.'

'I hate that guy.'

'Well you should because if you don't get your act together and do something brave, you'll lose her forever. Either to Wallace, or one of the terrorists bullets.'

'To be honest Rex, I think I lost her already. She's kind of mad at me.'

'Yes she is. But don't forget, it's Christmas Eve. A time for miracles.'

'I'm a big fan of Christmas miracles. God bless Christmas.'

Rex shook his head. 'Don't go thinking you're off the hook, numbnuts. You're going to have to rescue Flake and all the other hostages. That'll be this year's Christmas miracle.'

'Damn. Is it going to take long? I've got a cab booked for midnight.'

'It'll take however long it takes.'

Sanchez sighed. It sounded like some serious effort would be required. 'So what do I have to do?'

Rex pointed at the dead body of Klaus. 'First of all, let's use this guy to get a message to Flake. Let her know you're still alive, and you're coming to rescue her.'

Sanchez noticed Klaus's wallet poking out of his back pocket. He bent down and picked it up, hoping it might contain a staff card to use in any vending machines. It didn't.

'What are you doing?' Rex asked.

'Checking to see who these guys are.'

'They're just a bunch of disgruntled Italian fellas, don't worry about it.'

Sanchez pulled a driving license out of the wallet. 'This is fake,' he said. 'It says this guy is Mexican!'

'So fucking what!' Rex bellowed. 'Listen to me for a goddamn minute. We can use this guy to send a message to the other terrorists. Give 'em a scare.'

'But he's dead. How will he pass on the message?'

Rex took a deep breath. He looked irritated. 'First of all, take off your jumper and put on this guy's bullet proof vest.'

'But this is my best jumper!'

'Do you want my help or not?'

Sanchez decided it was best not to argue and started to pull his jumper over his head. It didn't come off easily. The damn thing seemed to have shrunk quite considerably. As he wrestled with it like it was an octopus, Rex asked him a question.

'You still got that gold hip flask she gave you?'

'How do you know about that?'

'Have you still got it?'

'Yeah.'

'Give it to me.'

'Will I get it back?'

'Of course.'

Ten

'In one minute I will kill another hostage!' Marco Banucci shouted for everyone to hear. 'Does anyone wish to speak up and tell me where Tiny Tim is? One minute!'

Flake agonized over what to do. Her conscience wouldn't allow her to give up Tiny Tim, but if she didn't then even more people could die. Thinking about it made her feel sick. She toiled with the idea of raising her hand, but every time she started to lift it she chickened out.

'Ten seconds" Marco announced. 'Nine… eight…. seven….'

Before he made it to "six" Marco was interrupted by the now all too familiar sound of Candice screaming. The elevator doors had just opened and she was staring into the lift with a look of horror painted across her face. Marco rushed over to see what had got her so shaken up. Flake (and everyone else for that matter) tried to get a good look inside the elevator. Marco was blocking the view though. Whatever he had seen in there certainly had him spooked.

'Bingo!' he yelled. 'Get over here, quick!'

One of the other terrorists, a guy with a long blond ponytail, wearing a black polo-neck sweater and a pair of brown chinos raced over to Marco's side and stared into the lift carriage. Flake tried to get a look around them to see what they were looking at. Eventually, through Bingo's legs she caught sight of another dead body in the elevator, only this time, it wasn't a hostage, *it was one of the terrorists.*

Klaus was propped up against the back of the elevator. His body was a bloodied mess. And his neck had been broken. The sight would normally have made Flake's stomach turn, but the relief that it wasn't Sanchez or Tiny Tim brought a smile to her face instead, particularly when she noticed that someone had used a black felt pen to draw a pair of comedy glasses and a moustache on Klaus's face.

Marco stepped into the elevator and leant down over his dead comrade. He pressed his hand against Klaus's neck to check

47

for a pulse. Flake knew he was wasting his time. She'd seen enough corpses during her time in Santa Mondega to know one when she saw one. Marco quickly recoiled and stepped back out of the elevator. He was clearly shaken. He turned to Bingo.

'I'm sorry,' he said. 'Your brother is dead.'

There was a strange moment of silence that followed, where the world seemed to stop spinning for a moment as Bingo took on board the news of his brother's demise. Then, right on cue he went apeshit. He started ranting and raving, banging his machine gun against the wall and cursing loudly in a foreign language. Marco attempted to calm him down by placing a hand on his shoulder, but Bingo shook it off and stormed over towards a potted plant in the corner of the room. He lifted his machine gun over his head and smashed it down on the plant pot, breaking it in two and spraying dirt everywhere.

Wallace nudged Flake. 'I've seen that jumper somewhere before,' he said, nodding at the dead guy in the elevator.

Flake took a look and instantly recognized the jumper. She wondered how she hadn't noticed it before. It wasn't the one he had been wearing when he had gone upstairs. It was the very same jumper she had bought Sanchez for Christmas a year earlier. It said "*I thought you'd be bigger*" on it in red lettering.

To Flake's surprise, Marco wasn't reacting angrily like his friend Bingo. In fact he wasn't even paying any attention to his irate friend's "plant-trashing" exploits. Instead he was sniffing his fingers and frowning as if he had discovered something foul under his fingernails. Flake's heart soared. She recognized the look on Marco's face. She'd seen it a hundred times before.

She leant over and whispered into Wallace's ear. '*He's still alive.*'

Wallace looked at her, bewildered. 'He looks dead from here,' he said glancing across at Klaus's body in the elevator.

'Not him,' said Flake. '*Sanchez.*'

'Sanchez? That loser boyfriend of yours? How can you tell?'

'Watch this,' said Flake nodding at Marco who was still sniffing his fingers.

Marco stared hard at his index finger for a second then put it to his lips and licked it. He immediately pulled a face and recoiled in disgust. 'Oh my God!' he yelled. 'It's *piss!* Someone killed Klaus and *pissed on him!'*

This was the cue for Bingo to storm off down the corridor towards Flake's office, screaming and yelling in his native tongue.

Wallace grabbed her arm. 'If your boyfriend really wasted that terrorist then he's going to get us all killed. What does he think he's doing?'

Flake smiled. 'He's doing what he does best.'

'Killing people?'

'No, *annoying people*. That's what Sanchez does better than anyone I've ever met. Trust me, only Sanchez can piss someone off that much.'

'You mean to tell me he pissed on a dead terrorist in order to annoy the others? Where's the sense in that?'

'It's a message,' Flake replied, her heart racing with excitement.

'A message for the terrorists? Telling them what? Mess with me and I'll urinate on you?'

'No. It's a message for me.'

Wallace scratched his head. 'Huh?'

'He's letting me know he's still alive and he's coming to get me.'

Eleven

'Was it really necessary to empty the *entire* hipflask over that guy?' Sanchez asked as he followed Rex up a flight of stairs to the eighth floor.

'I thought you liked pouring piss on everything? Rex replied.

'I do,' said Sanchez, 'but I usually leave a little bit in the flask in case of an emergency.'

'What? In case you get thirsty?'

'No. In case I bump into someone I don't like the look of.'

'You're a fucking weirdo Sanchez, you know that?'

'That's rich coming from someone who disguised himself as a Yeti.'

Rex stopped on the landing outside the fire door to floor eight. He looked at Sanchez and raised his eyebrows. 'I bet *you* wish you had that Yeti outfit now, don't you?' he said.

He had a point. Sanchez was now without his jumper, and was feeling the cold somewhat because he had just a white string vest to keep his upper body warm. It wasn't a good look. For a moment he wished he had some tattoos like Rex who had a cool *Psycho Killer* tattoo on his right bicep. Sanchez stared at it and wondered if it would look good on him.

'What's that tattoo about?' he asked.

Rex put his finger to his lips to warn Sanchez to be quiet. He nudged the fire door open and peered through it to make sure the coast was clear.

'What's here?' Sanchez whispered, peering over Rex's shoulder.

'A security office with a bunch of televisions.'

'Televisions? That's handy. I think *Weekend at Bernie's* is on.'

Rex didn't seem to be listening. 'Follow me,' he said. 'I've gotta show you something.'

Rex walked through the fire door and into a large office space. Sanchez followed, staying as close as possible to his giant buddy. If there was any danger lurking around, the safest place to be was close to Rex.

He followed the giant wrestler over to a small office in the corner. The door was open. Inside was a wall of monitors and two black leather chairs. Rex walked in and pointed at the monitors as if he thought Sanchez wouldn't notice them otherwise. The screens showed live video footage of all the floors in the building.

'This is the security office,' said Rex. 'All the CCTV cameras around the building are beamed into here so that security can spot anything unusual going on. I've been up here watching events unfold all day.' He pointed at one of the black leather chairs. 'Sit your fat ass down,' he ordered.

Sanchez did as he was told and sat on the chair. Thankfully it was extremely comfortable, and even more pleasing, it had wheels on it. Sanchez had visions of rolling around the office on it, pretending to row it like a boat. Unfortunately Rex was standing directly behind him so it wasn't possible. Rex placed his large metal hand on the back of the chair, as if he knew what Sanchez had in mind. He pointed at one of the monitors in the middle.

'Watch this,' he said. 'I've compiled a montage of todays events.'

'Oh good,' said Sanchez. 'I love montages.'

Rex pressed a button on the bottom of the monitor and Sanchez watched some footage from earlier in the day. It was a recording of Flake sitting behind the desk in her office. She had a framed photo of her and Sanchez on the desk, taken from their brief spell together in the Santa Mondega Police Force. He remembered the time well (wearing a police uniform and busting crime with Flake had been an absolute riot). Flake picked up the photo and stared at it for a while. She looked sad.

'See,' said Rex. 'She's remembering the days when you and her had fun together. Before you became a boring idiot obsessed with serving piss to people you don't like. Remember when you and her were cops? You were really heroic then. That's

51

how Flake fell in love with you. And look at what you've become.'

'In case you hadn't noticed,' Sanchez retorted, 'there aren't any vampires or werewolves in the city any more, so there's not much call for the kind of bravery I displayed back then.'

'Look,' Rex pointed at the screen again. 'This is Wallace presenting her with the golden hip flask. He's making her feel special. Miyagi should have presented it to her, but Wallace insisted on doing it, because he wants Flake to see how much he likes her. That's something you've been forgetting to do. That's your main problem, you've forgotten to remind Flake that you care.'

'She knows how I feel about her. Why should I have to keep reminding her?'

'You shouldn't *have* to Sanchez. You should *want* to. You didn't even remember to get her a Christmas present. Then you asked for *her* hip flask. Let's face it, you're selfish. You think only of yourself.'

'That seems a tad harsh.'

'Look, I'm here to help you out. Not that you particularly deserve it, but one thing I know about you is that for reasons that don't particularly make sense to me, people seem to *like* you and they want to see you happy.'

'Now that I *can* believe.'

'Good. Now watch this.' Rex tapped the screen to emphasize something important was coming up.

The monitor showed Flake in one of the building's corridors. She was walking alongside a small kid who was wearing a weird green velvet suit.

'That kid is fucking tiny!' said Sanchez.

'Yeah. That's Tiny Tim. He's the kid that the terrorists are after. Flake took him to a private cinema room. He's in there now, watching a movie.'

'Great,' said Sanchez. 'We can hand him over to the terrorists and collect the reward.'

'Don't make me hit you with my metal hand.'

'Huh?'

'You're not handing the kid over.'

'Why not?'

'Have you listened to anything I've said?'

Sanchez caught sight of something else on the monitor, a giant green tree. 'There's a Christmas tree there with loads of presents under it!' he gasped.

'Those are for the local orphans.'

'Yeah, but if I could snag one of them, I could give it to Flake.'

'You are unreal.'

Sanchez's cell phone began vibrating in his pocket. He pulled it out and looked at the display. The name NIGEL POWELL was flashing.

'You'd better take that,' said Rex.

Sanchez answered it and put the phone to his ear. 'Hello. Nigel?'

It sounded like Nigel was in a busy place because Sanchez could hear vehicles and lots of voices.

'Hey, buddy,' said Nigel over the background buzz. 'I'm down on the ground outside. Listen carefully. The cops have started showing up. Word is out about the terrorist takeover. People have reported hearing gunshots, and thankfully you had the good sense to make a call to emergency services. I'm now trying to convince them that you've got a hold of the situation. Do you know how many terrorists there are?'

Rex mouthed the word "Seven"

'Seven,' Sanchez replied. 'Although I've already bagged one of them. Broke his neck.'

'Really?'

'Oh yeah, big time.'

'Wow,' Nigel sounded surprised. 'Well done, I'll let the guys down here know that. Listen, for now, I'm gonna have to keep your identity secret to protect the people you care about. Don't give out your real name to anyone on this frequency, or talk about anyone you know because the terrorists have a hacking device that enables them to listen in on any phone calls that take place inside the building.'

'You sound really paranoid,' said Sanchez.

'Maybe so, but just do as you're told anyway. I want you to sit tight for now. I'll get the cops to take over from here. I think everyone will be very pleased when they hear about you killing one of the terrorists.'

'It was nothing, really,' Sanchez boasted. 'I take down bad guys all the time.'

Sanchez caught sight of Rex rolling his eyes. He clearly disagreed. Nigel seemed impressed though.

'What do you know about these terrorists?' Nigel asked.

'Well their fashion sense suggests they're from a Hollywood eighties movie, but their accents are definitely Italian.'

'Italian? Are you sure about that?'

'Well I checked this one guy's driving license and it said he was Mexican, but it's clearly a fake ID.'

'All right, look, I'll get the cops to take over from down here. You stay here.'

The voice of another man crackled onto the line. Sanchez recognized it. It was the terrorist Marco Banucci. 'Well, well isn't this nice?' he said, his voice dripping with sarcasm. 'Who exactly are you my interfering friend? I take it you're the guy that thought it would be funny to drench a dead guy in urine. Pissing on dead people is really low you know!'

'The comedy glasses and moustache was a nice touch though, eh?' Sanchez replied with great pride.

'You prick,' Marco sneered. 'I bet you're just another TV addict who's seen Lethal Weapon too many times and thinks he's Martin Riggs, aren't you?'

'Wrong again. I was always rather partial to Scarface actually.'

'Listen to me,' Marco snapped, clearly tiring of the banter. 'If you deliver Tiny Tim to me, I will let you live. There will be no repercussions. I will not look for you. I will not try to track you down. That will be the end of it. But if you don't, I will search this entire building for you, I will find you, and I will kill you.'

'Yes well, good luck with that, Mr Banucci,' said Sanchez.

'Aah, so you know my name. Care to tell me yours?'

'Nope.'

Rex snatched the phone from Sanchez and ended the call. Sanchez was about to complain, but Rex pointed at one of the monitors.

'Look,' he said.

On the monitor Sanchez saw a couple of Marco's henchmen stepping into the elevator.

Rex hauled him out of the comfy leather chair. 'Sanchez, it's time for you to get out of here. Those henchmen are on their way up here. I want you to run up to the next floor. That's where you'll find Tiny Tim. And remember, don't try to do a deal with these guys. Once they've got Tiny Tim, they'll kill everyone else. You understand?'

Rex held out the machine gun he had snagged from Klaus. 'Take this and go up via the stairs.'

Sanchez took it. It was a shitload heavier than Rex made it look when he held it. Sanchez tossed the strap over his shoulder and let the gun hang by his side. It made him feel pretty cool. Kind of like BA Baracus from the A Team, but white, and without the Mohican. Or the shit jewellery.

'Get moving!' Rex yelled with a degree of urgency.

Sanchez hesitated. 'What are you gonna do?'

'I'm gonna bag me some more terrorists. When they're dead I'll send 'em back down to Marco in the elevator. You can take the credit for it later.'

'Don't forget to draw some comedy glasses on them.'

'Of course. Now get going,' said Rex, pulling two handguns from within his sleeveless denim jacket and checking to see if they were loaded.

'Thanks. It was good to see you again Rex.'

'You too. Now fuck off!'

Sanchez dashed off towards the fire exit. He heard the elevator arrive in the hall behind him as he stepped out into the stairwell. He paused a moment to listen for any voices. What he heard was the sound of Rex shouting some crazy inaudible shit, and then opening fire on the terrorists. That was Sanchez's cue to get the hell out of there.

Twelve

The effects of the cocaine Wallace had snorted in Flake's private bathroom were beginning to wear off. His addiction to the white powder was so intense that he could barely function without snorting a line every half hour. The stress of the terrorist takeover had heightened his anxiety and the only thing that was going to help him through it was a line of coke. There was just one problem. He'd left his stash in Flake's private bathroom.

'I can't take any more of this,' he muttered to himself.

Flake was sitting beside him on the floor in the middle of the group of hostages. 'Shut up,' she whispered back, through gritted teeth.

'I'm not kidding. I can't just sit around here waiting for your friend Sanchez to get us all killed.'

Flake tugged at the sleeve of his jacket. 'You're not going to do anything stupid are you?' she asked.

'Don't worry,' said Wallace tugging at his shirt collar. 'I'm just going to get myself some coke, that's all.'

There were currently only three terrorists watching over the hostages. Marco Banucci and Bingo had disappeared off somewhere. So Wallace saw this as his opportunity to take a toilet break and help himself to another line of coke. He raised his hand and caught the attention of one of the remaining terrorists, a slimy looking fella with a big black perm and a red headband, clearly a Rambo wannabe who actually looked more like John McEnroe. The guy walked over, his gun primed and ready for use if Wallace tried anything stupid.

'What do you want?' he asked.

Wallace couldn't exactly tell him he needed a line of coke, but he needed to get to Flake's bathroom. 'I need a shit,' he whispered in reply.

'Too bad.'

'Seriously. I had a vindaloo earlier. I'm not kidding, if I shit myself here, you're gonna have to move everyone to a different floor.'

The terrorist pondered the idea for a moment. 'All right,' he said. 'Come with me.'

Wallace stood up and headed off towards Flake's office. The terrorist with the headband followed closely behind him, occasionally prodding him in the back with his machine gun to remind him of his predicament.

When they arrived at Flake's office, Wallace opened the door and strolled in. The office wasn't empty like he'd expected. Marco Banucci was sitting behind Flake's desk and his ponytailed buddy Bingo was perched on the edge of it. The two of them were discussing something in private and looked surprised to see Wallace walk in.

'Who are you?' Marco asked.

The henchman behind him answered. 'Some guy who needs a shit!'

'Well he's not shitting in here!' said Marco, a look of disgust on his face.

Wallace raised his hands defensively. 'It's a big one. I'm desperate,' he said.

Marco shook his head. 'I don't care.' He nodded at Bingo. 'Kill him. I'm not having him taking a dump in here while we're trying to catch the idiot that killed Klaus.'

Bingo stood up and pointed his machine gun at Wallace.

'Wait!' said Wallace. 'I can help you. The guy upstairs who's killing your friends, I can give him to you!'

Marco eyed him suspiciously. 'You know who it is?'

'Yes. His name is Sanchez Garcia. He's a bartender at the Tapioca.'

Marco reached out and grabbed Bingo's gun to prevent him from firing it. He lowered it so that it was no longer pointed at Wallace.

'What's your name?' he asked.

'Wallace.'

'And how exactly are you going to give Sanchez Garcia to me?'

'If you let me go and look for him, I can convince him to give himself up.'

'I'm not going to do that, because you'll run off and I won't see you again.'

'Well how else can I bring him to you?'

'Easy,' said Marco holding up a walkie-talkie. 'You can speak to him through this.'

'How would I do that?'

'We're hooked into the networks in this building. Next time your friend Sanchez makes a call, we'll cut in.'

Thirteen

Sanchez had taken refuge behind a giant Christmas tree on the top floor of the building. His plan was to hide there and let Rodeo Rex kill all the terrorists for him. It sounded like Rex had successfully killed a couple of them on the floor below because the gunfire had ceased. Sanchez felt nervous being on his own, not knowing if Rex was coming back or not, so he took out his cell phone and called Nigel Powell. The phone rang six times before Powell answered it.

'Sanchez, I'm kinda busy,' he said.

'Well excuse me! What's going on down there? Are the cops coming in, or what?'

'The Chief of Police is here,' Nigel said, lowering his voice. 'Some guy called Richard Williams. I think he's on to me because I'm not a real cop. And the FBI might be coming. Let me call you back.'

'Wait!' Sanchez yelled. 'I'm all alone up here and all I've had to eat is a Twinkie. Can you order me a pizza or something? Fat Frank's deliver any time, any place.'

Before Powell could answer, a second voice butted in. Marco Banucci's.

'Sanchez Garcia,' he said. 'I'm sorry to interrupt your conversation, but I have someone here who wants to speak with you. A very dear friend of yours from the party.'

Sanchez felt his blood run cold. If Marco had found out about his relationship with Flake she could be in serious danger. So it came as a huge relief to him when the next voice he heard on the line wasn't Flake's.

'Hey Sanchez, it's me.'

Sanchez couldn't mask his surprise. *'Wallace?'*

Wallace sounded quite chirpy and upbeat. He certainly didn't sound like he was in any danger.

'Hey buddy,' said Wallace. 'Listen up. The cops are here now, so you gotta stop killing terrorists. I need you to hand yourself in, or they're gonna kill me. They promise they won't hurt you if you surrender now.'

'Wallace, what have you told these people?'

'I told them we're good friends and that I could talk you into giving yourself up.'

Sanchez needed to shut Wallace up before he did anything stupid, *like mention Flake.*

'Wallace, put Marco back on.'

Wallace didn't do as he was told. 'Sanchez, would you get on board here?' he snapped. 'The cops are here now. You're causing more problems than your solving. This would all be over now if it wasn't for you.'

'Wallace, shut up. Put Marco back on.'

It sounded like Marco snatched the phone out of Wallace's hand. His voice came through loud and clear, and more threatening than ever. 'So Mr Garcia? Are you going to hand yourself in, and save your friend's life?'

'Not a chance! Marco, this guy is no friend of mine. Have you seen his haircut? The guy's a dick. Shoot him. See if I care!'

Sanchez hoped that would be the end of it and that Marco would tell Wallace to get lost before the conversation turned to Flake. Wallace though, wasn't giving up easily. He shouted into Marco's phone.

'Sanchez, how can you say that? After all we've been through?'

Sanchez pondered what to do. Wallace had the potential to seriously fuck things up. As he considered his options he could hear Wallace still babbling on to the terrorists but he was beginning to sound desperate, as if he realised he'd gotten in over his head.

Marco's sneering voice came back on the line. 'Mr Garcia. I am going to count to three and then I am going to shoot your friend in the face.'

Wallace chimed in. 'Hey Sanchez, buddy, come on man, they're pointing guns at me now!'

BANG!

The gunshot came through the phone loud and clear. Sanchez pulled the phone away from his ear for a moment. No further gunshots followed. After a few seconds Marco Banucci spoke again.

'Did you hear that Sanchez? Your friend is dead.'

'I thought you were going to count to three?' Sanchez replied.

'I was going to, but your friend Wallace was really irritating.'

'I told you he was a dick.'

'Maybe so,' said Marco. 'But there are plenty more hostages here for me to kill. Sooner or later I'll get to one that you really *do* care about.'

With that Marco hung up the phone. The line didn't go dead though. Sanchez could hear Nigel Powell in the background arguing with the Chief of Police, Richard Williams, a man Sanchez had met during his brief stint as a Police Officer. He listened in on Powell's conversation with Williams to see if he could pick up on any plans the cops might have for a rescue mission.

'Did you hear that?' Chief Williams said. 'Your friend Sanchez just let him die. Gave the guy up. Even called him a dick and said he didn't care if they killed him.'

To Sanchez's surprise Powell stuck up for him. 'Sanchez used to be a cop you know. He's one of us!'

'He was never a real cop,' said Williams. 'He filled in for about two days.'

'Well that should count for something.'

'Jesus Christ Powell, he's a *fucking bartender for Chrissake!* But what are *you?* I've never seen you before. Are you even a real cop?'

Sanchez got bored of listening to them bickering and decided it was time to hang up. He slipped his phone back in his pocket and thought about the consequences of Wallace's death and decided that maybe it was a good thing. In fact, there didn't seem to be a downside to it. Wallace was an asshole and got what he deserved, and now he was out of the picture, Sanchez's chances of getting Flake back had increased significantly.

He stepped out from behind the Christmas tree and peered around. There were flashing lights visible outside so he headed over to the window to see how many cops were on the ground outside. He took one step before he tripped on something beneath his feet. He looked down and saw a pile of Christmas presents wrapped in shiny gold paper. He'd kicked one of them a few feet across the room. He picked it up with the intention of putting it back under the tree. It was reasonably heavy. He shook it and it rattled gently. Now Sanchez wasn't generally one for opening other people's presents, but the label on this particular one indicated that it was to raise money for the local Sunflower Girls, and, well, Sanchez didn't like those little girls much, so he decided to open it. He ripped off the paper and saw that inside was a box containing a child's toy gun.

'What are you doing?' a voice from behind him asked.

Sanchez dropped the box and spun around. Standing in front of him was young boy in a creepy green velvet suit. He was aged around ten or eleven years old. But this kid was really small, maybe only two feet tall.

'Are you Tiny Tim?' Sanchez asked, pointing his machine gun at him.

The kid raised an eyebrow. 'You figured that all out on your own? Well done!'

Sanchez took an immediate dislike to Tiny Tim. 'Listen you little gimp,' he snapped, hoping to garner a little respect from the child. 'Do you have any idea what's been going on here?'

'Is that a machine gun?'

Sanchez had almost forgotten he had a machine gun hanging from his shoulder. The little kid was probably dead impressed by it.

'Yeah, it's a machine gun. What about it?'

Tim's eyes lit up. 'Wow. Can I hold it?'

'No you bloody well can't. You need to find somewhere to hide. There's terrorists in the building and they're looking for you.'

'Looking for me? Why?'

'Look kid, I don't want to alarm you or anything, but from what I can tell, they want to kill you.'

Tiny Tim's face turned a deathly pale colour. He began sniffing and it looked like he might be about to cry. The last thing Sanchez needed was a hysterical midget kid on his hands.

'I'm just kidding,' Sanchez lied.

Tim was breathing erratically as if he were about to have a seizure. 'Why would they want to kill me?' he spluttered, his voice quivering.

'I don't know, maybe because you're annoying,' Sanchez suggested. 'Honestly I was just kidding. No one is trying to kill you.'

'Why would you make a joke like that?'

Sanchez remembered the present he had just unwrapped. He reached down and retrieved it from the floor. 'Here, I got you this toy gun,' he said. 'It's a game of pretend. We're pretending that there are terrorists in the building. You and me have to hide and then shoot them.'

The lie seemed to work perfectly. Tiny Tim's face lit up at the sight of the box containing the toy gun. The colour returned to his face and he snatched the box from Sanchez. 'Wow! This is the best present ever!' he beamed.

The kid clearly didn't get a lot of presents. He tore open the box and yanked the gun out. He was obviously impressed by it, even though it was nowhere near as good as the real machine gun Sanchez had.

'Can I fire it now?' Tim asked, pointing it at the Christmas tree.

'Not yet,' said Sanchez. 'First we have to play a practice game of hide and seek. You go up to the ninth floor and hide somewhere where no one will find you. I'll count to a hundred and then come looking for you. Just make sure you stay hidden and don't come out if you see any Italian terrorists.'

'That sounds like fun!' beamed Tim.

'Good. I'll start counting. Go!'

Tim hurried off towards the fire exit. Sanchez figured it would be easy to find him because little kids are shit at hide and seek, so he took his eyes off the young lad and used his cell phone to call Nigel Powell. Nigel answered immediately.

'Sanchez? What's up?'

'Hey Nigel, I've just found the little kid that the terrorists are after. He's on his way up to the ninth floor. What should I do now?'

Powell's voice came through loud and clear. 'Sanchez, have you lost your fucking mind?'

'What do you mean?'

'I mean, the terrorists are wired in to hear any calls made in or out of the building. You've just given up what floor the kid is on!'

Fourteen

Marco Banucci watched Bingo drag the dead body of Wallace out of the office and down the corridor. Shooting the annoying, smug coke-head in the face had been one of the day's highlights. Unfortunately it had left a bit of a mess. There were specks of blood all over the walls and on the desk where Marco was sitting. He'd enjoyed killing Wallace. The guy was a slimy asshole so it was fun watching his brains spill out everywhere. In fact, Marco had enjoyed it so much he'd got an erection and had no intention of standing up any time soon in case anyone spotted it. He'd always found killing folks to be a bit of a turn on. There was something about it that just sexed him up.

He grabbed a box of tissues and wiped a few drops of blood off the desk phone. A big splodge of blood had landed on a framed photo too. The photo was of two cops, one male and one female. The male officer was a tubby fellow, and his face was concealed by a big chunk of Wallace's blood. The female was a fairly sexy brunette in a dark blue outfit, reminiscent of Heather Locklear in TJ Hooker. As Marco studied her face, he realized he recognized her. She was one of the hostages in the main hall. She'd been sitting next to Wallace. Seeing as how no one was around, Marco gave himself a quick rub under the desk as he looked at the picture. The image of blood sprayed over a hot chick in a cop outfit was very arousing.

His inappropriate rubbing was interrupted by the sound of feet pounding on the floor as someone hurried down the corridor towards his office. Seconds later Bingo burst back in.

'Boss, I got news!' he said, his voice full of urgency.

'What is it?'

'It's good and bad. Which do you want first?'

'I don't care.'

'Okay, well Fredo and Santino are dead. That Sanchez guy must have wasted them. Their bodies just came down in the elevator. Both of them have been shot in the head. Fredo's head is on backwards too. And erm, I don't know how to say this but...'

'But what?' Marco snapped.

'Santino's keychain is gone.'

Marco frowned. 'Meaning what?'

'He had the keys to the chopper.'

'The chopper? You mean our getaway helicopter?'

'Yeah.'

'Well, do we have spares?'

'We have two sets of keys boss.'

'Who's got the others?'

'Santino had both sets on his key ring.'

Marco put his head in his hands. 'How the fuck did this happen?'

'Well, you said we needed a spare set. I guess nobody thought we needed to keep both sets of keys separate.'

'Goddamn it. You said the news was good and bad. Which part of this was good?'

'None of it.'

'No shit.'

'The good news is, Paolo intercepted an outgoing call. This Sanchez Garcia guy is on the eighth floor and he's sent Tiny Tim up to the ninth.'

Marco jumped up from his seat and picked his gun up from the desk where he had placed it after shooting Wallace in the face. 'Then what are we waiting for?' he said. 'I'll take the stairs to the eighth floor and get my keys back from this Sanchez asshole. You take the elevator up to the ninth. That way there's no way either Sanchez or the kid can sneak past us.'

'Sure thing boss. When I've got the kid I'll come down and meet you on the eighth floor. Keep that Sanchez guy alive. I want him for myself!'

'I'll see what I can do. On your way out tell the others to stay put and keep an eye on the hostages.'

'You got it.'

Marco headed out of the office and rushed through the fire exit into the stairwell. He raced up the first flight of stairs taking them two at a time. As he approached the landing for the eighth floor, he slowed down and began edging his way up, his gun aimed at the fire door, half expecting it to fly open at any moment.

He stopped outside the fire-door. He took a deep breath and reached for the handle with his free hand.

THUD!

Without warning the fire door flew open and smashed into him, knocking the gun out of his hand. He watched helplessly as it flew over the bannister on the stairs and plummeted all the way down to the ground floor.

Fifteen

When Sanchez realised he might have given up his and Tiny Tim's positions on the airwaves he decided to make himself scarce before the terrorists showed up.

He hurried over to the fire door and charged through it. To his surprise he crashed into a man on the other side. The impact knocked something out of the guy's hand and over the stair bannister. The guy was wearing a smart grey suit and looked stunned at the sight of Sanchez standing in front of him with a machine gun hanging over his shoulder. Even though the man wasn't wearing chinos and a polo neck sweater, Sanchez had to consider the strong possibility that he was one of the terrorists. One of them had been wearing a grey suit when they killed Mr Miyagi. Sanchez hadn't seen the guy's face, only heard his Italian accent. To be on the safe side he pointed his machine gun at him and tried to look tough.

'Oh my God,' the man stammered in a dodgy accent that sounded a bit Irish. 'You're one of *them* aren't you?'

'Shit no,' Sanchez replied. 'I'm into chicks.'

'What?'

'Yeah, I like ladies. I'm not gay.'

The man looked confused. 'That's not what I meant. I meant, you're one of the terrorists aren't you?'

'Eh? Oh, no. I'm Sanchez.'

Sanchez inwardly breathed a sigh of relief. This guy was obviously not one of the bad guys. He was too nervous and he had an Irish accent not an Italian one. He had to be one of Flake's colleagues who had somehow escaped from the party, just like he had.

'You're not a terrorist then?' the man said, nervously.

'No. I'm just a guest from the party. Who are you?'

'My name is Buck. I'm a guest at the party too. My wife works for the company. I was looking for somewhere to hide.'

'Oh, right. Nice to meet you Buck,' said Sanchez. 'Now listen up. We can't hide here. I think the bad guys are coming to this floor.'

Buck looked around fearfully. 'Shit, really?'

'Yeah. We should head up to the next floor.'

'What's up there?'

'The little kid that these terrorists are looking for. I sent him up there to hide.'

'Okay,' said Buck. 'You lead the way then, seeing as you're the one with the machine gun.'

'Sure.'

Sanchez squeezed past his new buddy and made his way up the stairs to the ninth floor with Buck following behind. He opened the fire door on the ninth floor and checked to see if the coast was clear. The ninth floor had been transformed into a giant games room. Flake had spoken about it and Sanchez had wondered if it was really as good as she had described. Well it definitely was. It had a bowling alley and several pool tables and arcade machines dotted around. But what caught Sanchez's eye most of all, was a row of vending machines full of soft drinks, sweets and sandwiches. He waved Buck through and followed him in.

'I tell you what,' said Buck, looking around. 'These Japanese companies sure do know how to make a cool staff room, don't they?'

'Yeah,' Sanchez agreed. 'But they won't let you use cash to buy anything in here. You need a staff card to get anything out of those vending machines.'

'Are you hungry then?'

'Fucking starving.'

Buck pointed at Sanchez's machine gun. 'Shoot the glass on the vending machine with your gun.'

'What?'

'Shoot the glass!'

'But won't that alert the terrorists to where we are?'

Buck scratched his chin like he was deep in thought. 'Good point. Why not just smash the glass with the butt of the gun then?'

'That's a much better idea.'

Sanchez pulled the strap over his head and walked over to a vending machine that was full of sandwiches. He lifted the machine gun up and smashed it against the glass. It made a loud thudding sound, but the glass didn't crack even a little. All that happened was that Sanchez got a nasty vibrating sensation all up his arm.

'Ow. Fuck!' he cursed. 'This glass must be made of metal, or something.'

'Here. Let me try,' said Buck.

Sanchez handed him the machine gun. 'Careful, it really vibrates when it hits the glass,' he said.

Buck didn't use the gun to smash the glass, instead he ploughed the butt of it into Sanchez's stomach. It knocked the wind right out of him. Sanchez doubled over and fell back onto his ass, holding his stomach and wincing. Buck stood over him, a sneering grin on his face.

'How on earth did you manage to kill Klaus and the others?' he asked. His accent had suddenly changed. He now sounded Italian. This was Marco Banucci.

'It wasn't me,' Sanchez pleaded, holding his hands up defensively.

'Well that doesn't matter now, does it?' said Marco. He reached into his suit jacket, pulled out a CB radio and spoke into it. 'Bingo, did you find Tiny Tim yet?'

There was no reply.

'Bingo? Bingo? Are you there?'

'Maybe he's taking a shit?' Sanchez suggested.

'Shut up!' Marco pointed the machine gun at Sanchez's head. 'I've no need for you any longer, Mr Garcia.'

Marco squeezed the trigger. Instead of a loud bang, what followed was a rather impotent clicking sound. He squeezed it again. 'No bullets!' he snapped. 'You've used up all the bullets in this gun, you fucking idiot!'

Sanchez raised his hands defensively. 'I haven't even used it, honest!' It crossed his mind that it was an incredibly fortunate stroke of luck that the gun wasn't loaded. And quite a cliché too.

Marco looked infuriated. He squeezed the trigger again, as if he were somehow convinced it might start firing.

BANG!

Suddenly the machine gun flew out of Marco's hand and smashed into the vending machine. He staggered back and shook his hand like it had been stung by something. He looked confused.

Sanchez saw an opportunity to escape. He rolled over onto his front and started crawling away.

Something strange had happened and Sanchez couldn't quite work out what it was. Why had Marco's gun flown out of his hand? Marco knew why, because he ran off towards the fire exit, kicked the door open and vanished through it.

A voice behind Sanchez spoke out. 'You okay, buddy?'

Sanchez recognized the southern drawl on the man's voice immediately. He rolled back over and sat up. He found himself looking up at one of his favourite people in the whole world. A guy he hadn't seen in quite some time. A guy who was supposed to be dead.

'*Holy shit!*' Sanchez gawped. '*Elvis?*'

'Correct on both counts,' the King replied.

Sixteen

Sanchez loved Elvis. The guy was a legend. Cooler than cool. And he was always well dressed. His outfit of choice for the current situation was a shiny red suit with white tassels running down the sleeves of the jacket and a pair of matching red pants. He had a black shirt underneath his jacket, which was only buttoned up halfway, and a whole bunch of tacky gold chains around his neck. And as always, whatever the weather, or time of day, he was wearing his gold rimmed sunglasses.

'What you doin' here, man?' Sanchez asked.

'I'm the ghost of Christmas yet to come.'

Sanchez felt an overwhelming sense of disappointment. 'Oh, *that* shit.'

'Yeah. And lucky for you I just wasted some terrorist called Bingo on the floor above.'

'Bingo?'

'Yeah. Dumb name huh?'

'Did you make any good jokes when you killed him?'

Elvis peered over his sunglasses. 'I didn't have time to. And surprising as it may seem there aren't actually any good pay off lines for when you kill someone called Bingo.'

Sanchez thought about it for a minute. 'You could have told him his number is up,' he suggested.

'Like I said. There aren't any good ones.'

'You could have shouted "house" when you killed him.'

'Oh shut up for God's sake!' Elvis grumbled, his voice revealing a degree of irritation. 'Bingo nearly got his hands on Tiny Tim. Lucky for you I got there in the nick of time and rescued the little fucker.'

Sanchez saw Tiny Tim poke his head around from behind Elvis left leg. The kid was so tiny he had concealed himself easily behind Elvis's flared pants.

'Nice work,' said Sanchez. 'I was thinking we could trade the kid to the terrorists to get Flake back.'

Elvis sighed. 'Sanchez, do you have any idea what will happen if the terrorists get their hands on Tiny Tim?'

'They'll let the rest of us go home?'

'No. Come with me. I'll show you.'

'Show me? How?'

'I've made a short film for you. It's a film about the future and what will happen to you based on the decisions you make tonight. You're at a crossroads in your life, Sanchez.'

'Do we really have time for this?' Sanchez asked. 'The terrorists know we're on this floor. Shouldn't we be getting the hell out of here?'

A deep booming voice called out from behind them. 'I'll deal with any terrorists that come up here!'

Sanchez looked round. Rodeo Rex had reappeared in all his denim glory and he'd found himself a giant Stetson hat to wear. He now looked even scarier than when he'd been dressed as a Yeti. He tossed a set of keys towards Elvis. The King caught them and stared at them.

'What's this?'

'I stole the keys to the terrorists helicopter. You and me are late for our next job, so I figure you can fly us out of here later.'

'Cool. I just gotta show Sanchez some stuff first. Can you look after Tiny Tim?'

'I'd love to,' Rex said, strolling up to them. He reached down and picked Tiny Tim up in one hand, then tossed him onto his shoulder. 'How you doin' Tim?' he asked.

'Never mind him!' Sanchez butted in. 'That machine gun you gave me had no bullets in it!'

Rex looked down at him. 'That's 'cause I was worried you'd do something stupid, like hand it over to one of the terrorists.'

'He did,' said Elvis, handing Rex a twenty-dollar bill.

Rex smiled and took the twenty. He held it up for Tiny Tim who was sitting happily on his shoulder. Tim gratefully accepted it, his eyes lighting up at the sight of such a large sum of money.

'Right then Tim,' said Rex. 'You and me are gonna go play on some of these arcade machines for a few minutes while Elvis shows Sanchez a short movie.'

'Cool!' Tim squealed.

Sanchez watched Rex walk off towards the gaming area with Tim on his shoulder. 'It's no use!' he called after them. 'You need a staff swipe card to operate any of those machines.'

Rex walked up to a race car arcade machine and kicked it with his boot. It immediately burst into life. He placed Tiny Tim in the driving seat and within seconds the lucky little bastard was having the time of his life racing against a bunch of other cars on the screen in front of him.

Elvis grabbed Sanchez by the shoulder and twisted him around, away from Rex and Tim. 'This isn't going to be easy,' he said.

'No shit. That kid's not even old enough to drive. He's bound to crash,' Sanchez agreed.

'I don't mean that,' said Elvis. 'I'm going to show you what will happen if you hand that sweet little kid over to the terrorists.'

'Will I get a reward?'

'No. It'll destroy your relationship with Flake.'

'What? Why?'

Elvis frogmarched Sanchez over to the door of the cinema room at the far end of the hall. 'That's for you to figure out.'

'Can you be a little less cryptic? Is Flake going to be okay, or not?'

Elvis opened the door to the cinema room and pushed Sanchez though it. 'I'll show you how it all plays out,' he said. 'Then I'll leave it up to you to decide what to do.'

Seventeen

Marco Banucci raced back down the stairs in a panic. He burst through a door onto the sixth floor and dashed into the main hall where the hostages were all still sitting on the floor. His last two henchmen, Paolo and Giovanni were standing guard, watching over their terrified captives. Marco knew that the pair of them would be very disappointed when they found out that Bingo was missing, *presumed dead.*

The hostages looked on fearfully when Marco charged in, struggling for breath. He did his best to compose himself and give off an aura of calm as he sidled over to Paolo. Paolo was always calm in a crisis and could usually be trusted not to overreact, unlike Giovanni. That was obvious to anyone who saw them. Giovanni looked like Rambo or John McEnroe with his crazy headband, whereas Paolo kept to a discreet black polo neck and a slick haircut that was more late-eighties than mid-eighties.

Marco whispered into Paolo's ear. 'We're in trouble. We're going to have to abort.'

To his surprise, Paolo recoiled in shock. *'What?* No fucking way! You promised me a million bucks. In fact, you guaranteed it.'

'Yeah, but that was before the cops showed up. Me, you and Giovanni are the only three left. There are undercover cops everywhere. They've got Tiny Tim and they've wasted the rest of our gang. And they've got the keys to the chopper too!'

Paolo grabbed Marco by the throat. 'Well then you'd better find a way of getting us out of here. And I still want my million bucks, no matter what.'

Marco took hold of Paolo's hand and pulled it away from his throat. 'All right, calm down. Let me make some calls.'

'Fine. Make some calls. But make them quick.'

Marco dashed off down the corridor to Flake's office. He charged in and reached for the phone on the desk. Before he could pick it up he spotted the photo of Flake and her fat friend in their police outfits. The blood that had been covering the face of the man had slid down the picture. Suddenly Marco could see the man's face clearly. He only needed one look at it to realise that all was not lost. He rushed back out to the main hall in a far more confident mood than he had left it seconds earlier.

'Yo Giovanni! You got a spare gun?'

Giovanni pulled a spare handgun from the back of his pants and threw it over to Marco who caught it and checked to make sure it was loaded. It was. *Fully loaded.*

He scanned the room until he found what he was looking for. It didn't take long to spot her. Sitting inconspicuously in the middle of the group of hostages was Flake. He pointed the gun at her and smiled.

'Flake Munroe, I'm so pleased to meet you. That's a lovely photo of you and Sanchez on your desk.'

Eighteen

Sanchez was extremely disappointed by the cinema room. He had expected a giant screen with rows of seats and a rear projector. What he actually discovered when he entered the cinema room was a reasonably large widescreen television and an old fashioned video recorder. There were no rows of seats, just a few sofas and beanbags scattered around.

'This is shit,' he groaned.

'Just sit down and quit bitching,' said Elvis, shoving him towards a black leather sofa in front of the TV.

Sanchez plonked himself down on the sofa. It made a loud noise that sounded like a fart and Sanchez quickly discovered that even the slightest movement would invoke a fart noise. He amused himself for a while trying to make some really loud noises until he spotted Elvis staring at him with a look of disapproval. Elvis wasn't one to mess with, so Sanchez got comfortable and stopped moving before Elvis lost his temper.

Elvis grabbed a remote control from on top of the television and sat down next to Sanchez. The sofa made a farting noise. Sanchez just managed to stop himself from sniggering.

'Don't fuckin' smirk,' Elvis growled.

'I'm not.'

'You're thinking about it though, I can tell.'

'Actually I was thinking it would be nice if we had some popcorn. Can you get us some?'

Elvis ignored him again. He pressed a button on the remote and the TV hissed into life. 'Watch this,' he said. 'You might learn something.'

A title card came up in red cartoon lettering. The film was called "IT'S A WONDERFUL LIFE"

'Looks promising,' Sanchez noted. 'Is this a cartoon?'

'Yeah. See that guy there,' Elvis said, pointing at a character on screen. 'That's you in the future.'

'I become a cartoon character in the future?'

'Don't be a smartass!'

Sanchez sensed that Elvis was in no mood for sarcasm so he decided to watch the cartoon and keep his jokes to himself, unless he thought of a really good one.

Up on the screen the cartoon version of Sanchez was walking through a graveyard. The character had grey hair and loose fitting clothes, nothing like the real Sanchez.

'I look very trim,' Sanchez said. 'How old am I supposed to be here?'

'This is five years from now,' Elvis answered. 'And you look slim because you no longer have Flake to make you breakfast in the mornings.'

'Why not?'

'Because the terrorists downstairs are going to kill her in fifteen minutes. And without her, you're going to end up losing weight.'

'Much as I'd like to lose weight, I'd rather have Flake. Is there any way we can stop this from happening?'

'Yes.'

'How?'

'You have to work that out for yourself.'

'If I hand over Tiny Tim and give the terrorists back the keys to their helicopter, will they let Flake live?'

'No, they'll kill her anyway. You have two choices, if you hand Tim over to the terrorists they will kill him. They will also kill Flake, and then you.'

'Well that's not an option then. What's the other choice?'

'You and Tim escape in the helicopter with me and Rex. Flake and the other hostages will die, but so will the terrorists when the police eventually storm the building.'

'These are the two shittest options ever! There must be something else we can do?'

'You keep using that word, Sanchez.'

'What word?'

'*We*. This is about *you* and what *you* have to do to save Flake.'

'But surely you and Rex can kill all the terrorists for me?'

Elvis shook his head. 'Our work here is done. It was up to us to show you the error of your ways and what the future holds for you.'

Sanchez huffed. 'But this is shit. You're supposed to show me how I can change and save Flake, surely?'

'We've done all we can. Me and Rex have been called to another job.'

'Another job? Who are you working for?'

'The Man in Red.'

'The who?'

'The Man in Red. Me, Rex and the Bourbon Kid all work for the Devil these days. We round up undead folks and send 'em to Hell. Me and Rex had the night off so we could come and help you, but we've gotta get going now. Sorry buddy.'

'But how am I going to save Flake on my own?'

Elvis stood up. 'You'll figure it out.'

On the television screen, the cartoon ended and the words "THE END" flashed up on screen. Elvis headed to the back of the room to go and find Rex. Sanchez stared at the screen and tried to think of a plan. Coming up with plans wasn't a strength of his, unless the plan involved running away.

As he was racking his brain trying desperately to think of a plan, he noticed the TV screen flickering in front of him. The badly animated and somewhat depressing cartoon about the future had ended. The image of Bruce Willis appeared on screen. Elvis had recorded the cartoon over the film *Die Hard*. The film had just restarted at one of Sanchez's favourite scenes. For a moment he forgot about coming up with a plan and instead watched a battered and bruised John McLaine facing down Hans Gruber with a gun taped across his back. Sanchez admired the way McLaine cracked a one liner to distract the bad guys while he reached for the gun without them noticing.

After watching McLaine gun down the two remaining bad guys, Sanchez jumped up from his seat. 'Elvis!' he yelled. 'I've got an idea!'

Nineteen

Flake's heart was racing and her mind was overloaded with incomprehensible ideas about escape. For the past hour she had dreaded the possibility of Marco finding out that she knew Sanchez. But now that he had, it was so much more terrifying than she had imagined. Sanchez had really pissed off this Marco guy. And now Marco was pointing a gun at her.

'You're coming with me,' he sneered. 'We'll go to your office and you can entertain me in your private bathroom, while your boyfriend listens in on the phone.'

'He's not my boyfriend,' Flake said in desperation.

'So what is he then?' Marco asked, yanking her arm and pulling her in close enough to him that she could smell his odious kipper breath. 'Husband? Lover? Brother?'

'None of those. He's just some idiot I used to work with on the police force.'

Marco stroked her cheek in an unpleasant, porno-foreplay kind of way. 'Nice try,' he said. 'But I know a lie when I smell one. You're our ticket out of here, bitch.'

'And I know bad breath when I smell it, fuckface,' Flake retorted.

Marco spun her around and pressed his body up against her back, and thrust his pistol into the bottom of her chin. Normally that would have had her full attention, but she was also aware of what could only be his erect penis pressing into her backside through his pants. The guy was seriously turned on.

'Have you got a boner?' she asked.

'Shut up!'

It seemed like everyone in the room had heard Flake's question because suddenly everyone was looking at Marco and most of them were staring at his groin area, without looking like they were. Even his two remaining terrorist buddies.

'He's got a boner!' Flake yelled out, sensing Marco's embarrassment.

Marco yelled at one of his comrades. His voice revealing a fair degree of irritation. 'Paolo!' he snapped. 'Come with me to the office down the corridor.'

'What for?'

'I want you to get hold of this Sanchez asshole on the phone and let him know that I have his girlfriend. We'll tell him if he doesn't hand over Tiny Tim and the keys to the chopper within two minutes, I'm going to kill her.'

'Now that sounds like a plan.'

Before Paolo had a chance to take even one step, Giovanni who was standing by the elevator, waved his hand in the air. 'Hold on,' he shouted. 'The elevator is coming down!'

Flake looked up at the digital display above the elevator to see if he was correct. Sure enough the elevator was on its way down. It passed through the eighth floor and then the seventh. She hoped Sanchez was coming to save her. And she really hoped he had a clever plan, for a change.

The sound of the elevator gears churning slowed and came to a stop as it approached their floor. Paolo hurried over to Giovanni and the two of them took up positions either side of the elevator with their firearms pointed at the doors, waiting for them to open.

Marco pressed his little handgun harder into Flake's chin. It seemed to work simultaneously with his erect penis, which pressed even harder into her backside. Danger seemed to really get this guy going. And as if sensing that Flake desperately wanted to see who was in the elevator he twisted her around so that she could see nothing, but could still feel his stiff dick against her back.

A moment later Flake heard two things. Firstly the elevator made its obligatory pinging sound to notify everyone that the doors were opening. A second later, right on cue, Candice screamed.

'What is it?' Marco shouted.

Flake heard Paolo mutter the words, *"What the fuck is that?"*

'What is it?' Marco repeated. 'And will someone shoot that woman who keeps screaming?'

'It's a giant beaver man,' Paolo replied.

'A what?'

Marco dragged Flake towards the elevator, keeping his gun pressed tightly under her chin. She managed to get a look inside the lift carriage. Just as Paolo had said, propped up against the back wall was the waxwork model of Beaverman, a little known super-hero character.

'Shall I shoot it?' Giovanni asked.

'Check it. See if there's a message on it or anything, but whatever you do, don't lick your fingers after you've touched it.'

Giovanni stepped inside the elevator and carefully approached the model of Beaverman. He reached out to touch its face, as if he'd seen something of interest.

And just like that, in the blink of an eye, Giovanni vanished. And Candice screamed. Again.

Giovanni didn't vanish in the conventional sense. It's just that he was there one moment, but then in the next, his feet were disappearing out of sight through the roof of the elevator. Flake replayed the incident in her mind. It had happened so fast. A length of rope with a noose at the end had dropped down through the service hatch. The noose fell around Giovanni's neck, tightened and then *something, or someone* with the force of a hurricane had dragged his body up through the roof.

Paolo backed away from the elevator, keeping his machine gun pointed up at the roof of the lift. It would be too risky for him to open fire in case he shot his buddy Giovanni, if indeed Giovanni was still up there. As the elevator doors began to close, Paolo looked back at Marco, his face showing signs of desperation. 'What the fuck's going on?'

'He's getting help,' Marco muttered. 'Someone's helping him.'

'You're being outwitted by Sanchez' Flake said, taunting him. 'How does it feel?'

Before Marco could answer, Flake heard the voice of Sanchez behind her. During the distraction created by the elevator incident, he had snuck in via the fire exit and made his way into the auditorium undetected behind them.

'Marco!' he called out.

Marco spun around, twisting Flake with him, keeping her close and using her like a shield in case Sanchez tried to shoot him. But when Flake laid eyes on Sanchez, she was surprised to see he was unarmed. In fact he looked as though he was surrendering. He stood some ten yards in front of them with his hands in the air.

'Where's my chopper keys?' Marco snapped. 'And where's Tiny Tim? Hand them over or your girlfriend gets it!'

'Don't do anything stupid,' Sanchez said. 'I've got your keys right here in my pocket.'

'Okay,' said Marco. 'Take them out slowly, or I shoot this bitch.'

Flake struggled in the hope of breaking free of his grip, but it was no use, he was far too strong. And besides, the more she wriggled the more aroused he seemed to become. The pervert.

Paolo walked over and took up a position by Marco's side. He pointed a pistol at Sanchez. 'So this is the guy who killed all our friends?' he said, his voice full of surprise and scorn. 'Can I kill him?'

Sanchez butted in before Marco could reply. 'Kill me and you'll never find Tiny Tim!'

Marco was intrigued. 'So you do know where Tiny Tim is?'

'Yep. I'll take you to him as soon as you let Flake go. Anything happens to her and you'll never find him.'

'If you're bluffing you'll die horribly,' Marco sneered.

'I'm aware of that.'

'Good. But first, you can throw us the keys to the chopper.' He leant his head towards Paolo and spoke in his ear without taking his eyes off Sanchez. 'If he does anything stupid, shoot him!'

Paolo closed one eye and seemed to line his pistol up, aimed at Sanchez's head. Flake watched on as Sanchez lowered his left hand and reached into the pocket on his pants. He pulled out a set of keys and held them up.

'Throw them to Paolo,' said Marco.

'Let Flake go first,' said Sanchez.

'Very well,' said Marco.

Paolo cleared his throat to grab Marco's attention. 'Yo Marco,' he said, softly. 'This guy's got something strapped to his back. I think it might be a gun.'

Marco hadn't expected Sanchez to try and double cross him, but Paolo was right, Sanchez did have something strapped around his shoulders.

'Sanchez I'm disappointed in you,' he said. 'If you have a gun taped across your back and you're thinking of shooting me with it, you're in *big* trouble.'

'I haven't got a gun taped to my back, I promise.'

'Good. So throw Paolo the keys and then turn around slowly to prove it. If you've lied and you *do* have a gun taped to it, I'm going to shoot you *and your girlfriend.*'

Sanchez swallowed hard. He held the keys up. 'These are those special keys aren't they?' he said.

Marco frowned. 'What?'

Sanchez threw the keys to the ground at Paolo's feet before replying. 'These keys are the kind that explode!'

Paolo looked down at the keys by his feet, then he looked back up at Marco. '*Exploding keys?*' he said, frowning. 'What's he on about?'

Flake took advantage of the distraction and elbowed Marco in the ribs. It loosened his grip on her enough for her to wriggle free and knee him right in the crotch. He let out a yelp of anguish and instinctively cupped his aching balls.

Flake dived to the floor to get clear of any gunfire. Marco doubled over and rubbed his injured dick, but straightened up again almost immediately, keeping his pistol trained on Sanchez, who hadn't moved.

From her spot lying on the floor Flake had counted to seven since Sanchez had thrown the keys. No explosion had followed. He'd obviously been bluffing. It had worked to a point because Flake was now out of Marco's grasp. But Sanchez was now a sitting duck, unarmed and with a very angry, and still visibly aroused, Marco Banucci pointing a pistol at him.

'What the fuck was that about?' Marco asked.

'Just a joke,' Sanchez shrugged. 'You can pick the keys up, they won't explode really, honest.'

Marco continued staring at Sanchez but turned his gun on Flake who was still lying on the floor. 'You're not funny,' he said angrily to Sanchez. 'Show me what you've got on your back. If it's a weapon, make no mistake I will shoot Flake in the face.'

Sanchez raised his hands above his head again. He looked down at Flake. He had an apologetic look on his face, one that she had seen a million times before when she's caught him doing stuff he shouldn't have been doing. 'Flake,' he said softly, 'I did all this for you.'

Marco released the safety on his gun to show he was ready to shoot Flake in the face. 'For FUCKS SAKE!' he yelled at Sanchez. 'Turn around NOW!'

'Okay.'

Sanchez finally did as he was told and began to turn around. Flake hoped to God he hadn't taped a gun to his back in an attempt to be clever. To her relief, he hadn't. He'd done something else. Something no other person in the world would have possibly considered.

In a baby harness that was hanging over his shoulders, Sanchez had Tiny Tim strapped to his back. And the little kid was holding a gun. The gun was nearly as big as the kid and looked like it weighed heavily in his hands. But almost in slow motion the young lad raised the gun up, pointed it at Marco Banucci and squeezed the trigger.

BANG!

The bullet hit Marco in the chest. Blood spurted out in all directions. He dropped his gun and staggered back into Paolo. As the gun clattered to the floor, Flake reached out and grabbed it. She pointed it at Paolo before he could re-aim his gun at Sanchez, and squeezed the trigger. Paolo never saw it coming. Flake unloaded on him. She kept firing and ploughed a good three or four into his chest as she emptied the chamber of bullets just to be on the safe side. When there were no bullets left she took stock of what she'd done. She was on her knees pointing a gun at a dead guy. All of her work colleagues were sitting in a group not far away, watching on in shock and awe. And Sanchez was the other side of her, with a gun-toting midget strapped to his back.

Flake took a deep breath and placed the gun on the floor. She watched Sanchez making a mess of unhooking the harness around his shoulders. Rather predictably Tiny Tim dropped to the floor in a heap, making a loud thud as he landed on his face.

'You okay down there, Tim?' Sanchez asked him.

'I nearly shot myself in the face, you idiot!' Tim replied.

Sanchez offered him a hand and hauled him to his feet. 'I'll take this,' he said, retrieving the gun from the young lad. 'Now gimme five you little shit. We did good, didn't we?'

Flake smiled as she watched the two of them share a high-five. Their moment of triumph was eventually halted by someone coughing nearby. It was Marco Banucci, the bastard wasn't quite dead yet. He was laid out flat on his back, taking in his last few breaths before death came for him. Sanchez picked up Tiny Tim and carried him on his shoulders over to Marco. Flake joined them as they loomed over the dying terrorist.

Sanchez smirked at Marco and pointed at the little kid he was carrying on his shoulders. 'Hey Marco,' he said, in a voice that was meant to sound like Al Pacino. '*Say hello to my little friend!*'

Marco coughed and spluttered uncontrollably for a few seconds, no doubt enraged by the torment of being outwitted by Sanchez and his annoying payoff lines. It looked like he wanted to say something, but before he could blurt any words out, he choked one last time, followed by a weird gurgling sound and then a loud fart. A second later he was dead. Flake grinned, amused by the thought that the last thing Marco ever saw was Sanchez's smug face standing over him, grinning inanely, with a midget on his shoulders.

Sanchez sniffed the air. 'I think he shit himself as he died,' he declared.

'You know, I could use a hug right now,' said Flake.

Sanchez needed no second invitation. He threw Tiny Tim off his shoulders again and the poor little midget kid landed face first on the floor again, this time calling Sanchez something far worse than an *"idiot"*.

In spite of her disapproval at Sanchez throwing a handicapped kid around like a basketball, Flake was willing to forgive him for just about anything right now. She flung her arms around his neck and jumped on him, wrapping her arms and legs around his waist. Sanchez lost his balance and fell back onto the floor, taking Flake down with him. She ended up sat astride him on the floor, a position they had been in many times before, usually after watching wrestling on TV and trying to re-enact it.

'You killed all the bad guys for me!' Flake beamed.

Sanchez shrugged like it was no big deal. 'Was there ever any doubt?'

She kissed him hard on the lips. 'Of course not.'

'Great. So you'll come back to the Tapioca tonight? I miss your breakfasts.'

'Is that all you miss?'

'Your lunches are pretty good too.'

Flake smiled. 'You're so stupid.'

'Yes I am. Now, if you'll get off me I've got a Christmas present for you.'

'Really?'

Flake climbed off him and allowed him to get to his feet. Looking around she noticed that all of the other hostages were hugging each other and thanking their lucky stars they were still alive. A bunch of them came over to thank Sanchez. Flake was happy to forget about receiving her present for a moment while she watched him rightly receiving the plaudits and congratulations for his incredible heroics.

As she watched him with great pride, she caught sight of two men down by the corridor that led to her office. For a brief moment she feared they might be terrorists, but on closer inspection she was sure she recognized them. One of them was a giant of a man dressed from head to toe in blue denim, apart for a black leather glove on one hand and a Santa hat on his head. He was carrying a large sack over his shoulder. His buddy was wearing a red suit with white tassels on the sleeves and pants and a pair of gold-rimmed sunglasses. Flake had met them both many years before when she'd worked as a waitress.

The two men walked up to her. Rodeo Rex took off his Santa hat and bowed his head, then winked at her. Elvis went a step further. He reached out and took Flake's hand, then he leant down and kissed it.

'Nice to see you Flake,' he said, stepping back.

'I thought you guys were dead,' Flake replied.

'It's a long story.'

Before Flake could ask Elvis about it, Rodeo Rex dropped the large sack he had been carrying onto the floor at her feet. He gripped the bottom of it and lifted it up to empty all the presents out onto the floor.

'Merry Christmas!' he bellowed.

Flake looked at the pile of presents. 'Did you find these underneath the Christmas tree upstairs?' she asked.

'Sure did,' said Rex.

'These are the gifts that our main customers sent in for the staff.'

'That's right,' said Elvis, picking one of the gifts up. 'And this one has your name on it.'

Flake reached out and tentatively took the gift. It was a flat rectangular shape, wrapped in shiny red paper. The label on it said –

TO MY FLAKE
MERRY CHRISTMAS
FROM SANCHEZ
XXX

Flake looked back over at Sanchez who was busy accepting pats on the back and kisses on the cheek from all the grateful hostages. She looked back down at the gift in her hand.

'Open it,' said Elvis.

Flake unwrapped the present. Just as she had suspected from the shape of it, it was a framed painting. But not just any framed painting. It was the picture of the Santa Mondega skyline that she had painted. The one that had sold for a thousand dollars to an anonymous buyer the day before.

'What is it?' Rex asked, peering down at it.

'It's a painting I did of Santa Mondega at night.'

'It looks nice,' said Elvis.

Flake pressed it against her chest and walked over to Sanchez who was in the middle of telling a group of people how he drew some comedy glasses on a dead terrorist. She tapped him on the shoulder.

'Where did you get this?' she asked, showing him the painting.

'I bought it yesterday in the online auction.'

'You mean you're the anonymous buyer who paid a thousand dollars for my painting?'

Sanchez looked confused. 'Well yeah, I love all of your paintings. I thought this one was really cool, so I bid for it. I thought you'd want to keep it.'

Flake grabbed Sanchez and planted a big kiss on his lips. 'Let's go home,' she said, 'I need to start preparing our Christmas dinner for tomorrow.'

Sanchez still looked confused, but the realization that Flake would be joining him for Christmas (and cooking the dinner) brought a huge smile to his face.

Flake felt someone tugging at her dress. She looked down and saw Tiny Tim staring up at her. 'Look what Sanchez got for me!' he squealed, holding up a plastic gun.

Flake smiled. 'That's nice, and far more appropriate for a boy your age than the gun you used to shoot Marco Banucci just now,' she said, ruffling Tim's hair. 'Promise me you won't ever get mixed up in Sanchez's crazy plans again. He always comes out smelling of roses, but one day you won't!'

'I can see why you like him,' said Tim. 'He's a really brave guy.'

'Yeah, he's something,' Flake replied.

If the evening had taught her one thing, it was that being with Sanchez was fun and no matter how much danger she was in, she would always be safe with him. Sure, he had his faults, but they were far outweighed by his good points. For a while she stood staring at her painting of the Santa Mondega night sky, alone with her thoughts, marvelling at how lucky she was to have Sanchez as *"her guy"*.

Her sentimental thoughts were eventually interrupted by the sound of Sanchez offering Tiny Tim a drink from his hip flask.

Twenty

'Look it's snow!' cried Flake as she and Sanchez stepped out through the front doors of Waxwork Tower and out into the cool night air.

The weather outside was frightful. It was snowing in Santa Mondega for the first time since Rameses Gaius's ill-fated attempt to take over the city. And it was freezing cold. In spite of that though, it was wonderful to be out in the fresh air again.

The car park was full of police cars, press vehicles, ambulances, a fire engine and an endless number of cops, news reporters and medical staff. On top of that it looked like half the city had turned up with their cell phones to try and film or photograph anything that looked remotely gruesome. Sanchez considered the possibility that stories of his heroics would be all over the internet already. He might even have to start up a fan page on Facebook.

All around them the other recently freed hostages were rushing over to their loved ones in the crowd. There was an awful lot of hugging and kissing going on. In fact it was probably the biggest outpouring of emotion Sanchez had seen since the time Wesley Snipes popped into the Tapioca for a drink and all the local vampires shit themselves and piled out through the exits. But most of all it reminded him of just how lucky he was to have Flake. He slipped his arm around her waist and squeezed her in tight.

Up above the building the sound of a helicopter taking off drowned out all the other noise for a moment. Flake pointed up at it and shouted into Sanchez's ear.

'Is that Elvis and Rex?'

Sanchez nodded. 'Yeah. They're leaving town in style.'

'Where are they going?'

'Elvis said they had another job to go to. It's something to do with the Bourbon Kid. I think it involved Frankenstein or Dracula or something like that.'

Flake waved to the helicopter as it flew off into the night sky. 'Isn't it dangerous to be flying a helicopter in this weather?' she remarked.

'It can't be any more dangerous than what we've been through tonight.'

'That's true.'

Sanchez spotted a police officer in full blue uniform making his way through the crowd towards them. It was Nigel Powell. He was smiling broadly, showing off his incredible fake white teeth. Sanchez waved at him.

'Who's he?' Flake asked.

'The ghost of Christmas past.'

The former hotel owner and now self-professed "ghost of Christmas past" walked up to them and shook hands with Sanchez.

'Sanchez,' he said, brightly. 'Congratulations on a job well done. Is this Flake?'

'Yeah. Flake this is Nigel Powell. He was my eyes on the ground tonight.'

Flake reached out and shook Nigel's hand. 'So pleased to meet you,' she said.

'You've got yourself a good man here,' Powell replied. 'Sanchez and his brave actions tonight have gotten us all out of a tight spot. I've been in Hell for a long time. But now thanks to Sanchez I'm gonna be absolved of all my sins.'

'Errr.... that's nice,' said Flake. She nudged Sanchez and whispered in his ear. 'What's this guy talking about?'

'He's an alcoholic,' said Sanchez.

'Oh.'

Sanchez turned back to Powell. 'Any chance of a ride home?'

Powell grinned and gestured for them to follow him. 'Your driver is already here. Some guy showed up just now and says you booked him earlier this evening. But don't worry, the police force will reimburse you for your cab fare.'

Sanchez looked at his watch. It was just past midnight. 'Of course,' he said, turning to Flake. 'I got a ride here earlier from some weird cab driver. I forgot I'd told him to come back.'

'You'd better hurry,' said Powell. 'Because he said he only had a five minute window. And that was about three minutes ago.'

Powell led them through the crowd towards the driver's car, a silver Chevrolet Impala that was waiting just past a bunch of police cars.

'Here you go,' he said. He was in the process of reaching out to open the back door for Flake and Sanchez when suddenly a familiar sound filled the air.

Candice screaming.

It came from somewhere behind them near the entrance to the building. And on this occasion it wasn't just a scream. She shouted some words too. Three words that struck fear into everyone.

'HE'S GOT A GUN!'

Nigel Powell reacted immediately. He reached for the pistol that was hanging on his belt, unholstered it and spun around in one swift move. Sanchez dived for cover, accidently knocking Flake to the floor as he did so. The pair of them landed in a deep pile of snow, with Sanchez on top of Flake, shielding her from any stray bullets that might come their way.

BANG!

Powell fired off one shot from his gun. A deathly silence followed before a woman's voice called out.

'That guy just shot Tiny Tim!'

Sanchez and Flake climbed to their feet and looked to see what had happened. On the steps that led down from the building's reception, Tiny Tim was lying on his back, holding his leg. Blood was spurting out from a bullet wound just below his knee. Next to him on the steps was the toy gun Sanchez had given him.

Sanchez looked over at Powell who was standing, wide-eyed, staring at Tiny Tim, his gun still pointed at the kid, aghast at what he had done. Sanchez reached across and seized Powell's arm forcing him to lower the gun.

'What have you done?' he asked.

Powell looked distraught. '*I shot a kid.*'

'Why?'

'He had a gun.'

'Yeah, but it's clearly a toy gun,' said Sanchez.

'Hell, man,' said Powell, shaking his head. 'It's dark. The gun looked real enough.'

Sanchez reached out and tentatively took the gun from Powell's trembling hand. To make matters worse, Police Chief Richard Williams came bounding over, his own pistol drawn and aimed at Nigel Powell. 'You're under arrest Powell,' he snarled. 'You've just crippled Tiny Tim. And from what I can tell, you're not even a real cop. This is a mistake you're gonna have to live with for the rest of your days.'

Unfortunately for Powell, Chief Williams wasn't the worst of his problems. Of far greater concern was the grinning face of a large black dude in a red suit who was standing in the crowd behind the Chief. Sanchez spotted him too and recognized him. He'd seen the guy many years earlier in Nigel Powell's hotel in the Devil's Graveyard, during some shitty singing contest.

The Man in Red minced up behind Chief Williams and tapped him on the shoulder.

'It's all right,' he said. 'I'll take care of this.'

'Who are you?' Williams asked.

'Special Agent Lucifer. FBI.'

'Well, I'm in charge here…'

'Not any more.'

The Man in Red clicked his fingers in front of Williams's face. Almost instantly the chief froze. His face drooped and his eyes suggested he had fallen into some kind of deep trance. Sanchez clutched Flake's hand and pulled her away as the smirking Man in Red sidled up to Nigel Powell and put an arm around his shoulder.

'Such a shame Nigel,' he said. 'Just when it looked like you'd found your redemption, you went and crippled a young kid. You're going to have to come with me, *again*.'

It looked like someone had reached into Powell's chest and ripped out his soul. His face had drained of all colour and his hands were still trembling.

'It's not my fault,' he mumbled. 'What's a kid doing with a toy gun at a crime scene. It's not fair!'

The Man in Red pointed at Sanchez. 'Take it up with him, he's the one who gave the kid the gun.'

Powell stared aghast at Sanchez. His jaw dropped open. 'You fucking idiot! After all I did for you!'

Sanchez shrugged. 'What? What did I do?'

The Man in Red steered Powell away to a white Limousine that had pulled up nearby. A waiting chauffeur who was dressed in a black uniform opened the back door and gestured for him to get in. Powell reluctantly climbed in and the chauffeur closed the door on him.

'That was weird,' said Flake.

Before Sanchez could reply, a couple of ambulance crew members dashed past them and over to the stricken body of Tiny Tim who was crying in agony. Sanchez overheard one of them say that Tim would live, but that he would be crippled for life, most likely in need of a crutch. It crossed his mind that Flake, (being the charitable and compassionate citizen that she was) might want to offer Tim some help, or even adopt him. But they only had about one minute before their driver left.

'Come on,' he said, drawing Flake's attention back to the car. 'I think we've had enough excitement for one night. Let's get out of here.'

They turned back to the Chevrolet Impala. As Sanchez reached for the door handle, he was distracted by the sight of an attractive young blonde lady in a sharp black suit bounding over towards them. She had a microphone in her hand and a cameraman hurrying along behind her, filming her every move.

'Mr Garcia,' she yelled. 'I'm from SMN. Can we have a quick word?'

Before Sanchez could say yes, Flake lashed out and punched the woman in the face. Now Sanchez had never seen Flake punch anyone before, but *Fucking Hell,* what a turn on that was! Flake knocked the reporter lady out cold with one punch. Her cameraman caught the whole thing on film. He was a nerdy looking young guy in a big blue puffa coat and a matching beany hat. He took one look at Flake and backed away leaving his female colleague on the floor, where she was slowly vanishing beneath the falling snow.

'Wow,' said Sanchez. 'That was completely unprovoked.'

'Yes it was,' said Flake. 'But it's on national TV. Now every woman in the world knows that if they try to steal my man, I'll knock them the fuck out!'

Sanchez pulled at Flake's arm. 'Come on, let's get you out of here before you beat anyone else up on camera,' he said. He opened the back door on the cab and stepped aside to let her in. Flake jumped in and slid over to the far side of the seat. Sanchez followed her in and closed the door behind him. It was a relief to finally sit back in comfort again. The leather seats in the cab were an absolute blessing after all the running around that Sanchez had done in the last couple of hours. As before, the blue tinted screen was up, making it difficult to get a good look at the driver, so Sanchez shouted through the speaker hole in the middle of the glass.

'The Tapioca please, my good man!'

The driver said nothing. But he'd obviously heard because he released the handbrake and pulled away.

'Wow,' said Flake, leaning forward to get a closer look through the blue screen at the driver. 'That's a really cool jacket. Where did you get it?'

The driver did not respond. Sanchez leaned across and nudged Flake. 'Don't worry about him. He's a bit weird. Doesn't speak much.'

Flake sat back and grabbed Sanchez's hand. She looked him in the eyes and smiled. 'You know what Sanchez. I learnt something really important tonight.'

'Yeah? What's that?'

'I don't want you to ever change. I love you exactly the way you are.'

'Me too,' Sanchez agreed.

'So what did you learn?' Flake asked. 'After everything you've been through tonight. You must have learnt something?'

Sanchez pondered the idea for a moment before answering. 'You know what? I can honestly say, I haven't learned a thing.'

Twenty One

The driver parked the Chevrolet Impala by the side of the road outside the Tapioca. Flake looked at her watch. It was almost half past midnight. It had been a long night and she was exhausted, although she had a feeling she wouldn't sleep. The whole day had been just too damned exciting. She was already looking forward to telling her friend Beth all about it over a coffee on Christmas morning.

'Driver, how much do we owe you?' she asked, pressing her head up against the speaker on the blue tinted screen.

Sanchez opened the car door. 'It's okay,' he said as he twisted his legs to get out. 'The cops have agreed to pay the fare. Tell the driver he can add an extra fifty bucks on for the tip.'

Flake watched him climb out, then she looked through the blue tinted screen and into the driver's mirror on the front windscreen. For the first time since she'd gotten into the cab she made eye contact with the driver.

She called out to Sanchez. 'Why don't you hurry on in and pour us some drinks. I'll be along in a sec.'

'Okay.'

Sanchez left the door open for her and hurried up to the front entrance of the Tapioca, almost slipping on some black ice outside the front door. Flake heard him mutter something about hating ice and then watched him fiddle with his keys in the lock for a few seconds before he finally got the door open and dashed inside.

She slid over the seat to the open door and jumped out onto the pavement. The snow beneath her feet was almost an inch deep already. Sanchez will be livid, she thought. He's going to have to get a shovel and clear up some snow in the morning.

She closed the car door behind her and tapped on the driver's window. The window was blacked out so that all she could see was a silhouette of the man who had driven them home. She tapped on the window again and a second later it began to wind down. She crouched down so that she could lean on the door frame and speak to the driver.

'Hi,' she said. 'Merry Christmas.'

The driver looked at her and almost smiled. Almost.

Flake kissed her fingers and then planted them on the side of his face. 'You look good,' she said.

The driver whispered back. 'You too.'

Flake shoved him playfully on the shoulder. 'So, have you got a message for Beth or what?'

The driver replied in a deep gravelly voice. 'Yeah. Tell her I'll be back, real soon.'

The End (maybe....)

18978480R00061

Printed in Great Britain
by Amazon